Praise for *Held*

'Anne Michaels' compelling novel *Held* couldn't be more timely: war and its damages, passed through generations over a century. Through luminous moments of chance, change, and even grace, Michaels shows us our humanity – its depths and shadows' Margaret Atwood

'A graceful, timely, resonant reminder of the trauma of war and the wreckage that it inflicts' *Daily Mail*

'A cleverly fragmented tale of love, memory, and time shuffles the hopes and dreams of four generations ... As strong and as meaningful as a finished monument' *Guardian*

'There is a lyrical beauty to this novel ... with Anne Michaels, you know you are in the presence of a real and rich sensibility' independent.co.uk, Books of the year

'Still a master of her universe ... The writing is always personal, hypersensitive and profoundly interior ... At the heart of this book lies the question of how goodness and love can be held across the generations' *Observer*

'Few authors balance the atrocities of history with the consolations of human relationships quite so effectively as Anne Michaels. She has an uncanny talent' *Financial Times*

'There is an intense, mysterious beauty that infuses Michaels' precise prose with a compelling power that is exquisite ... a profound literary experience that is executed with subtlety, grace and an exquisite intuition' *Irish Times*

'*Held* may be one of the most romantic books I've ever read ... Gorgeous ... Surprisingly expansive ... Hauntingly beautiful ... The whole novel is spiked with little detonations of awe ... Michaels publishes novels so deliberately that each one entrances readers of a new decade' *Washington Post*

ANNE MICHAELS' books have been translated into more than forty-five languages and have won dozens of international awards, including the Orange Prize, the *Guardian* Fiction Prize, the Lannan Award for Fiction and the Commonwealth Poetry Prize for the Americas. She is the recipient of a Guggenheim Fellowship and many other honours. She has been shortlisted for the Governor General's Award, the Griffin Poetry Prize, twice shortlisted for the Giller Prize and twice longlisted for the IMPAC Award. Her novel *Fugitive Pieces* was adapted as a feature film. From 2015 to 2019, she was Toronto's Poet Laureate. She lives in Canada.

annemichaels.ca

HELD

ANNE MICHAELS

BLOOMSBURY PUBLISHING
LONDON · OXFORD · NEW YORK · NEW DELHI · SYDNEY

BLOOMSBURY PUBLISHING
Bloomsbury Publishing Plc
50 Bedford Square, London, WC1B 3DP, UK
29 Earlsfort Terrace, Dublin 2, Ireland

BLOOMSBURY, BLOOMSBURY PUBLISHING and the Diana logo
are trademarks of Bloomsbury Publishing Plc

First published in Great Britain, 2023
This edition published 2024

A catalogue record for this book is available from the British Library

ISBN: HB: 978-1-5266-5911-8; TPB: 978-1-5266-6253-8; PB: 978-1-5266-5912-5;
EBOOK: 978-1-5266-5909-5; EPDF: 978-1-5266-5908-8

2 4 6 8 10 9 7 5 3 1

Typeset by Integra Software Services Pvt. Ltd.
Printed and bound in Great Britain by CPI Group (UK) Ltd, Croydon CR0 4YY

MIX
Paper | Supporting
responsible forestry
FSC® C171272

To find out more about our authors and books visit www.bloomsbury.com
and sign up for our newsletters

for
John Berger
Simon McBurney
Liz Calder
Alexandra Pringle
Rebecca and Evan

CONTENTS

I

RIVER ESCAUT, CAMBRAI, FRANCE, 1917

We know life is finite. Why should we believe death lasts forever?

*

The shadow of a bird moved across the hill; he could not see the bird.

*

Certain thoughts comforted him:

Desire permeates everything; nothing human can be cleansed of it.

We can only think about the unknown in terms of the known.

The speed of light cannot reference time.

The past exists as a present moment.

Perhaps the most important things we know cannot be proven.

He did not believe that the mystery at the heart of things was amorphous or vague or a discrepancy, but a place in us for something absolutely precise. He did not believe in filling that space with religion or science, but in leaving it intact; like silence, or speechlessness, or duration.

Perhaps death was Lagrangian, perhaps it could be defined by the principle of stationary action.

Asymptotic.

Mist smouldered like cremation fires in the rain.

*

It was possible that the blast had taken his hearing. There were no trees to identify the wind, no wind, he thought, at all. Was it raining? John could see the air glistening, but he couldn't feel it on his face.

*

The mist erased all it touched.

*

Through the curtain of his breath he saw a flash, a shout of light.

It was very cold.

Somewhere out there were his precious boots, his feet. He should get up and look for them.

When had he eaten last?

He was not hungry.

*

Memory seeping.

*

The snow fell, night and day, into the night again. Silent streets; impossible to drive. They decided they would walk to each other across the city and meet in the middle.

The sky, even at ten o'clock at night, was porcelain, a pale solid from which the snow detached and fell. The cold was cleansing, a benediction. They would each leave at the same time and keep to their route, they would keep walking until they found each other.

*

In the distance, in the heavy snowfall, John saw fragments of her – elliptic, stroboscopic – Helena's dark hat, her gloves. It was hard yet to tell how far away she was. He shook the snow from his hat so she might see him too. Yes, she lifted her arms above her head to wave. Only her hat and gloves and the powdery yellow blur of the streetlamps were visible against the whiteness of sky and earth. He could barely feel his feet or his fingers, but the rest of him was warm, almost hot, from walking. He pulsed with the sight of her, the vestige of her. She was everything that mattered to him. He felt inviolable trust. They were close now but could not make their way any faster. Somewhere between the library and the bank, they gripped each other as if they were the only two humans left in the world.

*

Her small ways known only to him. That Helena matched her socks to her scarf even when no one could see them in her boots. That she kept beside the bed, superstitiously unfinished, the novel she had been reading in the park the day they understood they would always be together. The paper-thin leather gloves she found in the pocket of the men's tweed coat she bought from the jumble sale. Her mother's ring that she wore only when she wore a certain blouse. That she left her handbag at home and slipped a five-shilling note in her book when she went to the park to read. The boiled sweets tin she kept her foreign change in.

*

Helena carried the handbag he had bought for her on the Hill Road, soft brown leather, with a clasp in the shape of a flower. She wore the silk scarf she had found in the market, made hers now by her scent, autumn colours with a dark green border, and her tweed coat with velvet under the collar. How many times had he felt that velvet when he held open her coat for her. A finite number. Every pleasure in a day or a life, numbered. But pleasure was also countless, beyond itself – because it remained, even only in memory; and in your body, even when forgotten. Even the stain of pleasure and its taunting: loss. The finite as unmanageable as the infinite.

*

They walked to his flat and left their wet clothes at the door. No need to turn on the lights. The blinds were up, the room snow-lit. White dusk, impossible light. John was always surprised, he never stopped being astonished, at how little there was of her, she was tiny it seemed to him, and so gentle and fierce he couldn't breathe. He had bought the scented powder she liked and he filled the tub. He added too much and the foam spilled over the steaming edge. 'A snowbank,' she said.

*

The young soldier was lying only a few metres away. How long had the boy been staring? John wanted to call out to him, make a joke of it, but couldn't find his voice.

*

Pinned to the ground, no weight upon him.

Who would believe light could fell a man.

*

John's child-hand in his mother's hand. The paper bag of chestnuts from the vendor with the brazier in front of the shops, too hot to hold without mittens. Leaning against his mother's heavy wool coat. Her smooth hand-bag against his cheek. Peeling the brown paper skins of the chestnuts to the steaming meat. The tram squealing on the track. The edge of his mother's apron escaping from the edge of her coat, the apron she forgot to take off, the apron she always wore. Trams, queues, the smells of fish and petrol. Her softness against his hard childhood. Her scent before he succumbed to sleep, the burnished warmth of her necklace as she leaned over to him. The lamp left on.

*

The inn had been built beside the rail tracks, next to the rural station, in a river valley. Long ago, the inn and the valley had been a tourist destination, promoted by the train company for its view of the mountains, the wildflower meadows, the aromatic pines and betony. The rail tracks were shadowed by the slow river, like a mother struggling to keep up with her child, silver lines running the length of the vale.

Helena had been heading for the larger town beyond, but had fallen asleep. She could not stop herself from drifting off, succumbing as if drugged by the motion of the train. And when the train stopped at the last station before the town, she had, half asleep, misunderstood the conductor booming out the next stop and had grabbed her satchel and disembarked a station too early.

Beyond the dim lamp by the exit, it was dark — profound country darkness. She felt foolish and slightly afraid; the deserted platform, the locked waiting room. She was about to sit on the single cold bench and wait for daylight, when she heard laughter in the distance. Later, she would tell him she heard singing, though John remembered no music at all. She stood at the exit, not wanting to leave the pitiful protection of that single dusty bulb in the station. But, leaning into the darkness, she saw, some distance away, the inviting pool of light of the inn.

Later, she would imbue the short walk in the darkness towards that corona of light – the endless fields of invisible grasses rustling around her – with the qualities of a dream; the inevitability of it, the foreknowledge.

Looking into the front window, Helena saw a room enclosed in a time of its own. An inn of legend, of folklore – warmth and woodsmoke. Faded upholstered armchairs, scarred wooden tables and benches, stone floors, massive fireplace, with a store of logs to last the coldest winter, stacked from floor to ceiling, the self-perpetuating supply of a fairy tale, each log, she imagined, magically replacing itself over the centuries. John watched as she sat down nearby. It was, to him, an encounter of sudden intimacy in this public place; the angle of her head, her posture, her hands. He watched as a man – soused and staggering, every careful step an acknowledgement of the spinning earth and its axial tilt – fell into the vacant chair opposite her, giving Helena a slow, marinated gaze until his head fell, weighty as a curling stone, and slid across the table. John and another onlooker jumped up to help at the same time and, between them, dragged the man to the back of the pub to sleep it off. When John returned, he found his own table taken by a couple who did not look up, already lost to the room around them.

'I'm so sorry,' Helena said, quickly gathering her coat and satchel, 'please, take this table.'

He insisted she stay. With a great effort past shyness, she asked if he would care to sit with her. Later she would tell him of the feeling that passed through her, inexplicable, momentary, not even a thought: that if he sat down she would be sharing a table with him for the rest of her life.

*

In the little window in the hallway, from the heat of the bath, they could see the snow falling.

*

The black lines of the trees reminded him of a winter field he'd once seen from the window of a train. And the black sea of evening, and the deep black bonnet and apron of his grandmother climbing up from the harbour, knitting all the while, leading their ancient donkey burdened with heavy baskets of crab. All the women in the village wore their tippie and carried their knitting easy to hand, under their arm or in their apron pocket, sleeves and sweater-fronts, filigree work, growing steadily over the course of the day. Each village with its own stitch; you could name a sailor's home port by the pattern of his gansey, which contained a further signature – a deliberate error by which each knitter could identify her work. Was an error deliberately made still an error? Coastal knitters cast their stitches like a protective spell to keep their men safe and warm and dry, the oil in the wool repelling the rain and sea spray, armour passed down, father to son. They knitted shorter sleeves that did not need to be pushed out of the way of work. Dense worsted, faded by the salt wind. The ridge and furrow stitch, like the fields in March when they put in the potatoes. The moss stitch, the rope stitch, the honeycomb, the triple sea wave, the anchor; the hailstone stitch, the lightning, diamonds, ladders, chains, cables, squares, fishnets, arrows, flags, rigging. The Noordwijk bramble stitch. The black and white socks of Terschelling (two white threads, a single black). The Goedereede zigzag. The tree of life. The eye of God over the wearer's heart.

If a sailor lost his life at sea, before his body was committed to the deep, his gansey was removed and returned to his widow. If a fisherman washed ashore, he was carried home to his village, the stitch of his sweater as good as a map. And once he was restored to home port, his widow could claim his beloved body by a distinctive talisman – the deliberate error in a sleeve, a waistband, a cuff, a shoulder, the broken pattern as definitive as a signature on a document. The error was a message sent into darkness, the stitch of calamity and terror, a signal to the future, from wife to widow. The prayer that, wherever found, a man might be returned to his family and laid to rest. That the dead would not lie alone. The error of love that proved its perfection.

*

There were rules of the sea that also applied to life on land and any sailor, knowing the changing face of the deep, was a fool to ignore a warning. If, in the early morning, on the way to the docks, a fisherman encountered a hare or a priest or looked into the face of a woman – even wife, daughter, sister, mother – he would not dare sail that day. Along the dawn streets to the North Sea harbours, women dutifully turned their backs to the men. And after death too, there were strict rules of passage. In the villages, the coffins were carried thus: fishermen bearing fishermen, women bearing women, land folk bearing land folk.

*

His father had given up the sea for the fields. Sailor or farmer, what kind of freedom had his father known, or his grandfather? The freedom of a man breaking his back to plant his own harvest.

When John remembered his father, he seemed only able to recall fragments – deep feeling, but only pieces – moments together, not even days. Years, an entire life – now only this handful, this heartful.

*

Stories told on a battlefield, on a life raft, in a hospital ward at night. In a café that will disappear before morning. Someone overhears. Someone listens, attentive with all his heart. No one listens. The story told to one who is slipping into sleep, or into unconsciousness, never to wake. The story told to one who survives who will tell that story to a child, who will write it down in a book, to be read by a woman in a country or a time not her own. The story told to oneself. The fervent confession. The meandering, repetitive search for meaning in a gesture, in a moment that has eluded the speaker's understanding for a lifetime. Stories incomprehensible to the listener yet received nonetheless – by darkness, by the wind, by a place, by an unperceiving or unperceived pity, even by indifference.

What we give cannot be taken from us.

*

It was late now. Outside the inn, there was only the dim light of the station and the stars beyond.

John could not explain what he felt – it seemed that he and Helena had been there before, that they were enacting something, that everything they spoke had been somehow fated. He felt that if he returned to the inn the next day, it would not exist, she would not exist.

He said he would wait with her until her train came. He wondered why she was not afraid of him, a stranger in this isolated place. He was a little afraid of her.

Inside the warm inn, they had talked about second chances. Outside, in the cool night, it seemed they had known each other always. He almost reached for her hand.

*

He would understand, later, that there is a moment when your life must become your own; you must claim it from all the other stories you've been given, that have been handed down or thrust upon you, or that you've been left holding while someone else claimed theirs. He already knew that the life unchosen, left behind because of cowardice or shame, does not wither. But instead, without exception, grows rampant, choking the path ahead.

It would be like stepping out of one's clothes, he thought. Like entering the sea, where you can no longer tell where your skin begins.

He had never considered before that drowning could be a gentle death. But perhaps the sea might be the best place to die after all. The sea, where, like memory – he had once written down – the elusiveness of the form is the form. Before this moment he would have said there was discipline in such mental detachment. Now he thought, when something is detached, it is broken.

*

Impossible to name the exact moment night falls, elusive as the moment sleep overtakes us.

*

The water he washed with stank in his helmet, a pool too filthy to hold a reflection. As if the dimmet itself were whispering, he could hear Gillies' voice. At first, he didn't know if Gillies was talking to himself or some-one else, but soon John understood that Gillies' words were meant for him. Somewhere along the way, they had thrown in their lot together. John had learned the

three kinds of twilight – astronomical, nautical, civil –
from his father, but in that place it was as hard to tell
the age of the dawn as to tell the age in a man's face.
Gillies was twelve years older than John and had already
been stitched up more than once. 'In the hospital at
Sarnesfield,' Gillies said, 'there was a nurse, the Miss
Ella Leather. She sang to us when the ward was dark,
with only a little lamp by each bed…'

The dawn was a kind of scum over everything.

*Oh no for another I will not seek, not as long as I do
live…*

*For I never never had but one true love, and he lies fast
asleep…*

'I won't say no one cried,' said Gillies.

*

Her breasts fit perfectly in his hands.

*

He felt a presence, a thermal current, a tremor across
the entire surface of things, like a heat mirage. A deepening, not a darkening. He knew he'd felt it because
immediately he felt something even more certain and
powerful: its dousing. Drowned by his clumsy incom-
prehension, his limitation, his twitch of doubt.

*

The snow in the dusk made him wonder if light was rising from the ground.

Would he know the moment of his death or would it be like night falling.

*

John's grandfather had been washed ashore and carried home to his village, restored by the pattern across his chest and the deliberate error in his sleeve.

All the sailors that summer who had washed ashore — Adrianus, Martinus, William, Jens, Arie, Thomas, Dirk, Joos, Hendrik, James, Luc, Dorus, Edward — and all the women of the North Sea ports who had earned a new title ahead of the family name: Widow Maris, Widow Fischer, Widow Langlands, Widow Martin, Widow Hansen, Widow Meijer, Widow Williamson, Widow Fairnie, Widow Troost…

Some maintain this is hearsay, that there is no evidence of sailors ever being returned home by way of a knitted cable crossing the wrong way. But, like everything we find hard to believe, it need only have happened once to be true.

*

Cold blows the wind o'er my true love, cold blows the drops of rain...

'I won't say no one died listening to her,' said Gillies.

*

Perhaps consciousness only occurred when there were enough humans alive to generate the spark, to seal the circuit, the critical mass for the grain of sand to become the dune, the synapse to allow a flock to change direction in an instant. There would be other metaphors later – the chiasmata, the interchange, the crossing over. The cable crossing the wrong way.

*

Is the soul in death, consciousness without matter?

There was that church near Siena with its gargoyle, a head with two bodies. Would it be more of a torment to have two heads with one body?

Everything, he thought, is dualistic, nothing is alone: the snow growing brighter only as dusk deepens.

*

It was snowing hard now, why did he not feel cold?

He remembered feeling pain. Why did he not feel it now?

*

The pub was almost empty; the drunken man who had brought them together, asleep still. John would wait with Helena at the station, hours yet before morning. Her chestnut hair gleaming, her tweed coat with its prim collar. She was graceful, earnest, searching, gentle, he did not know how to belong to anyone, how would he let her go.

'Pity doesn't give us any right over another human being,' she said, 'or give any human being a right over us.'

'It's a form of judgement,' he said.

'Pity isn't love,' she said.

Who had ever spoken to him this way?

'And mercy?' he asked. Mercy is another form of judgement, he thought. Bestowed...but still, a judgement. What is *agape* then? A surrender to the good.

*

'I can understand falling asleep and missing your stop, but who falls asleep only to get off the train too soon?' Helena laughed. And then suddenly she looked as astonished as he felt, as if an enchantment had brought her to this inexplicable place, sitting across a table from each other. How could events of such fragile chance feel exactly like inevitability? How many countless switch points had been necessary to bring them together at this table, this country night at the end of summer, under the ancient map of the stars, a map that had already passed out of existence, yet luminous and clear.

Faith uses the mechanism of doubt to prove itself. It is absence that proves what was once present. We can understand without proof, he thought, we can prove without understanding.

*

In the mudhole, no one had spoken, it seemed, for hours. Can you hear a man thinking in the dark? Yes.

'I can cover the moon with my hand,' said Gillies.

Snow fell on this field in the Iron Age, in the Bronze Age, on those buried beneath him, the distant trees like a runic Snellen chart. Soon, he thought, he would no longer be able to read the smallest line.

*

Where John and Helena waited near the train station, the road marker had been effaced by rain, each letter only the softest indentation, as if a finger were capable of erasing stone.

The night grew around them by degree, by slow permeation. Like sea fret, like love, that gradually soaks us through.

*

He would have to remember to write it in his diary, when he could reach his pocket, still a bit of pencil left: if you take the wrong road, you will never reach the meeting place.

*

What does a mother say to her child when he wakes in the night, his soul sick with fear? That he is safe in her arms, loved by her forever, nothing can end this love she holds him in, love without end. And he looks into her face, the face of unalloyed love, and slowly he lets this love suffuse him, and they fall asleep in each other's arms, old mother and grown son, separated by hundreds of miles.

*

Perhaps in death, he thought, we lose the details and keep only the feeling associated with those details. Is that what the soul knows in death – the separation of feelings from memory?

*

The tweed of her coat, the silk of her dress.

*

He came home from school to find his mother lying on the bed – never in all his life had he seen her lie down during the day. She was on her side; he saw her ribs and hip bone. She hadn't even taken off her shoes, the worn, black, lace-up shoes she always wore. He would never forget his tenderness and fear. She held out her hand and he lay down beside her.

How old had he been? Not more than twelve or thirteen. His father newly dead. Not much younger really than the young soldier watching him now, who he could almost touch, if he could only reach out his arm.

*

No escape from the pain of faith even in this darkness, even when belief is completely disassembled; if the parts could be fitted back together, would it be a lantern or a gun? Any word the heart speaks, even the bitterest renunciation or scorn, hangs in the air waiting for a response.

*

His mother fell asleep and, lying next to her, he listened to the rain. The warm summer rain, his mother often said, that made her want to run outside to feel it on her arms, to raise her face to it.

*

And if he died here? In this filth instead of the clean brine, without a gansey the colour of the night sea, soaked and clinging to his skin, cold and heavy as chain-mail, no one to recognise the error?

*

Meals in the small garden, rushing inside to undress, the next day finding their teacups in the grass, filled with rain.

*

The thin pale cotton of Helena's nightgown, worn sheer with sleep; the faint shadow of her bare legs.

*

The young soldier, not more than two arm lengths away, continued to watch him without speaking.

*

The shadow of the bird's folding and unfolding, like a silk scarf in the wind, wings against the sky like the turning of a page inside out, a message passing between them.

*

How alert the dead soldier looked, how absolutely, utterly awake.

II

RIVER ESK,
NORTH YORKSHIRE, 1920

Sunday morning, the bells tolling eternity. John forced himself to be still. Helena beside him, swimming in the river of sleep, her cotton nightgown riding up under her arms, her hair floating around her. The church at Hull, stained glass melted to liquid. The French in Reims wearing their Prussian-avenging red trousers. Frenchmen, trenchmen. The 450-mile-long grave.

*

John stood in their small kitchen as if lost. Helena had to ask him to sit down. His lame leg extended. He reached his hand to the light falling across the table. As if he could pick it up, she thought, as if he could not believe it.

*

The train hurtling home, eating into the future; its wake of smoke the burning away of possibilities, chances already extinguished. In each direction, torpor lurking behind every action, a draining of momentum in every decision. Fear so tirelessly attached to hope, it was hard to tell the difference between them.

*

Helena scrubbed clean the potatoes and carrots, chopped them, slid them into a pan. The innocent earth they'd come from.

She filled the teapot and sat down next to him. She took his hand.

'Does Mrs Harvey still live next door?' John asked.

'Yes,' she said.

'Is that her Jip barking?' he asked.

'Yes.'

She watched him take in this information, as if it were an instruction, as if he had asked for directions.

*

From the edge of the North Sea, twenty miles distant, a faint hum reached the stone ear, the acoustic mirror that faced the sea. The measured drone of an aircraft engine twenty miles away. Fifteen precious minutes' warning.

*

He had once possessed another faculty, a resilience he was only aware of now that it was gone, undetectable as a tide in a river; his father had told him of a boat that looked perfectly whole as it sank, weeping water from every seam. Invisible as the radio waves and cosmic rays that pass through us, the seiches and forces of history that restrict us, shape our assumptions, compassions, freedoms, judgements; the regrets of one generation passed down as hopes for the next, the germs and spores of limitation and expectation we absorb from the social atmosphere. How a bird struggling against the wind can appear motionless.

*

On his first Sunday home, they drove to Molk Hole. In the early mist, the chalk cliffs looked like icebergs. They watched the blizzard of birds, kittiwakes devouring their own questions, cries echoing against the cliffs. John held Helena's hand and felt the signet ring that had been her mother's, a hair's width of gold, like a pencil line around her finger. M for Mara; on her hand now, M for mother.

'We could run away,' Helena had whispered, before he'd joined up, next to him in the dark.

'Where would we go?'

Long silence. 'St Kilda.'

He'd laughed. 'We'd stick out like scarecrows.'

Even she had to laugh at herself, until indignant.

Now John knew he'd been wrong to laugh. He couldn't live without her fierceness for their sake, together. She had woken him in the middle of the night: what had conscription to do with them? Now, as she drew her hand to her hair to keep it back in the wind, he saw her nape bare above her sweater. All the secret softnesses he was allowed to touch. 'We could find a cave somewhere,' she'd plotted in the dark, 'we could hide the smoke from our cooking fire, we could live on nettles and forage the sea…'

Now they stood on the cliffs again. He could not understand how he had been so lucky – to be left for dead, gutted, thrown back.

*

While supper cooked, we built a house on the kitchen table with stones from the beach. Sometimes, down from the mountain, so tired from the climb, supper was soup from a tin, biscuits torn from a package, a square of chocolate by the fire. The house had once been a mill on a thread of water. We read to each other in the continuous sound of brook and sea, slept under blankets heavy as the night enclosing. What happened to the switchman's lantern, the stones on the table? Who reads my father's book of

Tolstoy's stories under the blanket? There was another house, a plank hut by a tarn, a bed, a table, a scrap of rug, a sink, a woodstove, the painted shutters, the childhood story told in the dark. Your blue shirt. The sea was as large as death, you said, its crashing so loud, even at the supper table we had to whisper. Mouths and ears. Stars like daylight through a weave of curtain. We've never lived far from the sound or sight of water. There was the worker's cottage in the town that aluminium built, and the pub in the middle of the field where we woke to frost on every filament and fibre, stalk, stave and stone, silver filigrees of microscopic precision. We found the road to the ruins at dusk. Biscuits, a flask of tea in the car. Our sleeves wet out the car window, washing our cups in the rain.

I'm writing this, John, not because I think you've forgotten, but because I know you remember.

*

Above the sea smoke, in the echo chamber of the cliffs, the persistent calls of the kittiwakes, as if hoping for a different answer. All along the coast, the stone mirrors, listening.

*

The photography studio, which they lived above, had been closed since the day he enlisted. Now he raised the blinds in the storefront and took stock of what was needed. John saw that Helena had painted and chalked new backdrops for the studio – a summer garden, a distant view of meadow and mountains, an Italianate terrace, a piano.

He did not have his strength yet and could not stand for long without his leg searing. Helena convinced him to hire an assistant, someone with experience who knew the chemicals and procedures, how to arrange the lights and props for maximum effect. Someone who knew about shadow. A ready man named Mr Robert Stanley.

'London's a big place and it was a small outfit... But perhaps you know it – Mr Sawyer's establishment in Exmouth Market.' Mr Robert Stanley looked at John with transparent eagerness.

'I'll write to Mr Sawyer for references.'

'Mr Sawyer didn't come back from France, sir.'

'Is there no one else to vouch for you?'

'No, sir. I learned everything from Mr Sawyer and worked nowhere else. Perhaps you could try me out for a few days – no pay – and see if I don't know my way around in the dark.' Mr Stanley grinned. 'See if I'll suit. Sir. Every man has his own way of doing things. I respect that, and I'm a quick study. You only need to say what you want once, and then I'll know.'

It was true. Mr Robert Stanley had considerable skill. He could light a scene as well as John could. Perhaps better.

Mr Stanley was from Pitlochry; why had he not returned home after his discharge? 'No family there now.' And why come here, to this little town? 'I had an aunt here I used to visit when I was young.' Happy memories? After a silence, 'Aye.'

Sometimes they would take a break and stand outside, smoking together in the meagre sunlight. John knew almost nothing about his assistant, except that he'd been a photographer's apprentice in London until he'd been called up. 'No service badge for me,' Mr Stanley said. Did that mean he'd attended an exemption tribunal and had been refused? Mr Stanley offered no further comment. John realised his assistant's reticence bothered him less than disclosure might have; it was, perhaps, preferable. The silence between them was not an intimacy, nor was it particularly amiable. But neither was it unfriendly. It was simply the acknowledgement of a relationship of mutual convenience, a desire to get on, with the least complication. Sometimes Mr Stanley would break the silence with not a comment or a question, but a statement, as if he were asserting something for the record, so there should be no doubt of, say, his support of the Triple Alliance or the Poplar Revolt. Often, John would not respond until a day or two later, after he'd had time to think, and only if he felt he had something to add. He would painstakingly craft his reply to be equally, or perhaps more, conclusive, and then drop his own pronouncement into the space between them: 'Ironically, no political system, no matter how crushing or reductive, operates without the basic premise of free will; for any system is dependent on the submission of that free will.' Or, 'Every time we disguise the truth, we weaken our will.'

Then Mr Stanley would give a characteristic brief nod, as if he'd scored the point himself, drained his pint and smacked his empty glass on the table. Once, by way of an answer, Mr Stanley had simply unbuttoned his jacket to show him a folded copy of *The Worker* in his breast pocket.

*

John remembered his grandfather's boots at the back door of his grandparents' house near Flamborough Head, two holes into which his own child-legs could vanish entire. Once, he woke early and saw the lamps already lit in the kitchen. He had thought his grandmother was praying but she was knitting. He would like to put his feet in those boots now and walk into the sea. He would like to leave his lame leg in one of those boots, dump it out with the panniers that had always been piled beyond his grandparents' back door, the stink of wet wicker, of fish in the rain, the sod of their garden pickled in sea brine. He'd saw off his leg himself if he believed it would stop the pain, but he knew it would never be gone, even when he was.

*

The towpath at the end of the overgrown garden led to the river; hanging willows, grass and sedge, the steady rapids that had once warmed the heart of a miller beyond the weir. Helena unfolded the blanket and John set down the basket in the shade. The water was cold and clear on their feet. He sat so long watching the light moving in the water, she wondered if he could perceive an order in it. Then he lay back, watching the willows moving against the clear sky until his eyes closed. The scent of sun-baked grass. Helena took his hand and placed it on her thigh; he felt the smooth strength of her under her flowered dress. When he thought about the soul, he imagined a state of abstract feeling – yet he could not imagine emotion un-attached to specific experience, unattached to the body, to Helena's body; is it possible to know something our body does not know? Are we born with feelings already in us, waiting to be recognised? Would terror uncon-nected to memory be purer, more potent, or would it be weakened by abstraction? A canteen sloshing with an inch of dirty water. If you were gagging at least you were breathing. Air an element capable of rotting. You see, he thought, I am still capable of orderly, accurate words like rotting, bilious, fester, putrefy…

'How lucky we are,' Helena whispered, no more than a breath – to herself, to the river, to the blessed day – so as not to wake him.

*

As a homecoming present, Helena had painted a scene on the shutters in their bedroom, so that even when they were closed, he could still see the gleam of the moon across the river.

*

He was surprised how quickly customers found him, and how eager they were for a family portrait.

They came wearing their best clothes. The men preferred to sit, disguising an amputation or a brace, others posed in profile to omit from view an eyepatch, scars, profounder disfigurements. John knew the necessity of these portraits for the wives and mothers – proof of homecoming, an argument for believing family life had resumed, evidence of various forms and degrees of survival and return. He himself would have either scorned the camera entirely or scorned the illusion, facing the camera with wounds on display.

He worked methodically, thoughtfully, grateful for the preparations and solutions, the ritual of it. That what was created by light was revealed by darkness. John had immediately appreciated Mr Stanley's almost furtive adeptness; he was inconspicuous and neat. John soon trusted that things would be found where he left them, especially in the darkroom. Yet, there were clues that Mr Stanley was a different man outside the studio – perhaps more than unruly in his opinions and his politics – not because he was unprincipled, but because of his principles. It did not seem that Mr Stanley's reserve was natural, but rather a product of discipline, his simultaneous acknowledgement of both the fact and superficiality of his subordination. Mr Stanley's obedience put John firmly in his assistant's power; it mocked him, intensifying its hold; it inflicted a complicity. The imbalance of power had been evident almost immediately – it was like recognising someone's handwriting; for a moment, as if he could see the shadow cast on Mr Stanley's features from within. John was not disturbed by this glimpse into Mr Stanley's character; took it instead as evidence of honesty, practicality. But he was wary of Mr Stanley's contempt.

They were setting up for a family portrait, unrolling the mountains and draping the table with a long cloth that would obscure the vanished limb of one of the sitters. The first time they worked together, John had brought out the cloth and explained what it was for – 'to hide what's invisible, and to hide what mustn't be seen'. He told Mr Stanley he would have preferred to photograph the truth – not to provoke pity, but to enrage.

Mr Stanley gave his quick nod – not in agreement, John knew, but in derision. 'We're not the lads with the tin faces, spending our days on the blue benches down in Sidcup.'

He knew he did not deserve Mr Stanley's dismissal. And if he could still think in terms of desecration and derangement, if he recognised the meaning of those words, then surely something in him was still sound. He wanted to answer Mr Stanley but held his tongue. He wanted to ask, if only it did not seem so self-pitying, how many parts can be taken from us before we are no longer ourselves.

*

He could still feel Gillies thinking in the dark, still woke to his voice. 'The way the Miss Ella sang,' said Gillies, 'pulled you from the edge, or pushed you over it.'

He had been startled by Gillies suddenly close, touching his sleeve, then thrusting something into his hand.

He felt the familiar shape of a carte-de-visite. It was too dark to see the image.

'That's my mother and me,' said Gillies.

'Where are your people from?'

'Abergavenny… But naught there now.'

'Have you a girl?'

John learned it was possible, even in the pitch-dark, to discern a man putting his head in his hands.

*

A neatly dressed young man was already waiting outside the studio when John came downstairs to unlock the door. He wanted his photograph taken to give to his father. His mother had died while he was in the war, he explained, and now he was leaving for a job away and his father would again be alone. John assessed the young man: straightforward standing portrait, perhaps holding a book, a simple backdrop of velvet curtains. He nodded for him to come in.

He inserted the holder with its negative into the camera.

'Will it hurt?' the young man joked.

'Only if you have something to confess,' John joked in turn.

The young man stopped smiling.

'A Lewis or a Vickers?' asked Mr Stanley, who seemed to appear from nowhere.

'Vickers,' the young man said, suddenly restored.

The question had immediately put the young man at ease. Why did it bother him that his assistant was so canny? Shouldn't he be glad of it?

'If I come back tomorrow, will it be ready?' the young man asked.

John nodded.

*

Helena painted a board until it was a square of night, or as close to what the dark looked like to her. And then, to all that expanse of darkness, she added a single drop of paint, smaller than the point of a pencil, the point of the light of a distant candle flame. Then she added an almost imperceptible gradation of radiance, at first glance only blackness. And she painted the infinitesimal gap between flame and wick, which might as well have been a chasm because nature dictates that a flame and its fuel source never touch. And then she became obsessed by that gap and painted it again in magnified detail, the space that allowed the flame to exist, the relationship of flame to wick no different than that of soul to body, tethered each by a breath.

*

They had been reading in bed. Their first night living above the studio, newly married. Helena had painted a grove on the wall behind the bed, so they could sleep under the trees. He leaped up and started down the stairs.

'What are you doing?' Helena had asked.

He came back with a broom.

'What are you doing?' she asked again.

He leaned the broom against the wall.

'So we can sweep up the leaves in autumn.'

She'd smiled and closed their bedroom door so he could see behind it, where she'd painted a garden rake so realistically he could see the wood grain in the long handle burnished by sunlight. She had thought of that sunlight, so it would glow even when hidden behind the open door.

He had taken her hand and they had gone back to bed, where he disappeared under the blankets to rest his head on the thin fabric of her nightgown, for which he felt an enduring tenderness, the nightgown that always vanished by morning.

*

If it had been an animal sound, a feral sound, it would have been less terrifying than that industrial throbbing, as if the clouds themselves had turned machine. The moon was a bright patch of haze, like the faint glow of a distant detonation. The throbbing seemed to come from one's own skull and through one's body, like the buzzing cable of premonition.

*

His mother had gone to live in Halesworth and sometimes Helena had joined her there, a place that seemed as quiet as one could hope for in those days of urgency, sinking dread, inertia. To visit Helena and his mother on leave and then return again to duty was a transition so unreal it should have turned him mad; it would have been better to lose one's mind than to retain that residue, enough left of oneself to spatulate and sift the madness, like a chemist frantically seeking the antidote to his own poisoning.

But then, in an instant, there would be no dissonance between leave and return, no meaning to it at all.

*

From below, a boy saw two red eyes in the clouds. He jumped onto his bicycle and tore down the London Road to Theberton, where a pilot – in his pyjamas, enjoying a cup of tea before bed – also heard the humming sky. While the gaze of those terrifying eyes followed the rail line to Halesworth and passed Saxmundham, the pilot took to the air still in his dressing gown and dropped his barrage. For seven eternal minutes, all anyone could hear was the rushing sound of the flames, as the Zeppelin drifted down to crash into a cornfield near Eastbridge, one skeletal end thrusting out of the ground, looking not like something that fell to earth, but like a whale breaching the surface of the sea.

*

'We could wear everything we own and leave in the middle of the night,' Helena had said. 'There must be places to hide – the Hebrides, the Shetlands…Foula… How long would it take to walk somewhere, to disappear? If I had the courage, I'd bash you on the head or drug your tea and kidnap you. We could disguise our trail, we could live with the sheep—'

'You don't love me enough to bash me with a frying pan?'

'Don't laugh at me.'

He had heard the river from their bed; he had imagined the magnesium light of the moon, its fractured light, and had felt, soaking into his shirt, her hair still damp from their swim.

*

I do not know where you are or what you see when you look up at the sky and we say our goodnight. (The same moon at least.)

Your mother came and we floated on the river in her gift. In all my life, I never imagined the glory of a rowing boat for a wedding present or such a dear mother-in-law to know me so well. By lucky chance my friend Ruth Lloyd and her little girl have moved not too far from your mother, and Ruth had the excellent idea of inviting your mother to her, or sometimes vice versa, so now I can visit them both in a single day, sometimes staying with your mother overnight before taking the train back. Ruth has fallen in with your mother too, who is so taken with Ruth's daughter that Ruth now visits her without me. So, your mother is having lots of company and she is never alone too long.

Last night I waited until very late then bathed in the river in complete privacy, except for Jip, who lay on the bank and watched, his swaying tail flattening a patch of grass. The water was cold as snow, though I was thinking of you and felt warm.

*

I'm bunking in with your mother, so we can both have company and so I can be near Ruth to help out with her little girl when the new baby comes.

It's the next day — I'd hardly arrived at your mother's when Ruth said it was time, I'm back on the train for Ruth's now and I'll finish this letter from there...

Ruth's aunts and sisters are here and the whole Lloyd sisterhood looked at the new baby in wonderment — a boy — the first in the family since Ruth's great-great-grandfather! Everyone worships him on sight...

*

He remembered Helena's hands in her lap, unsure if she should wait for someone to come round or to order her tea from the barkeep, unsure of the customs of that new land, the rural pub on the rail line, the flower still in the buttonhole of her coat, from, he would later learn, the garden where she and Ruth had their picnic to celebrate the first birthday of Ruth's daughter. Ruth, the first of Helena's school friends to have children, the friend she clung to, a bond he would later witness as if looking at a work of art he couldn't understand, something to be respected, something of unerring beauty. Not many things are unerring, he thought, and they deserve our acknowledgement if not our awe.

*

Above Halesworth, only a fraction of a second had passed; all the time it takes for an accumulation of events to overcome an entire world, for something to become irrevocably lost, separated from its original meaning: a photograph or a diary in the ruins, gazed upon by strangers. Lost, along with the privacies that form the real biography, never recorded or known; the countless inner adjustments we make to be in the world, to accommodate our loneliness, our ache for reunion.

*

The sky was completely black, yet the river, like aluminium, shone. My bare legs and arms were chilled by the early darkness. There was continuous lightning but not a drop of rain. For almost two hours the water was perfectly still. Then, for one isolated moment, the leaves stirred and the surface was a single shimmer — only to become motionless again. There was suspense now in that still surface, something alive and present, yet without breath. A ghost. In the black sky, a small hole appeared, and inside, a few stars. Slowly, the hole grew to the night expanse. The starlight was bright and the spasms of lightning continued, but all night not a drop of rain.

*

Helena had thought of hiding together in a cave, maybe in one of the Flamborough coves, but the coast was already a defensive line, with its stone mirrors. Or Scotland maybe, in the hills, learning to build a cooking fire no one could see, and living off lichen and salmon until the plague of conscription had passed. She had thought of pretending he was colour-blind, daft, she had thought of wrapping his head in bandages and saying he was concussed. Instead, he went when he was called up and did live underground, and did learn to make a smokeless fire.

'The water in my helmet is so filthy it could kill a fly,' said Gillies, who had no one, no siblings, no parents, no girl. Why not sign up? Nothing says you belong more than a uniform. Gillies hated having to fall asleep in daylight, as if that were the biggest crime against nature he could assimilate in that place.

*

John had been unreasonably affronted that their explosives came all the way from Canada – a wild place he had imagined untouched and clean – a fact that seemed aimed to destroy yet another fantasy he had not even been aware of in himself. One overheard such things in the dawn, before sleep. Next to him, Gillies, who always looked for one of the dogs to sleep next to, once told the story of his uncle who'd been cheated by a business partner and lost everything, and who, when he became senile in old age, kept asking for the betrayer, begging to see him, believing him to be an old friend, remembering only that they had been intensely connected, but not the nature of that connection. 'Can you fathom it?' Gillies asked anyone who happened to be listening, 'can you fathom not remembering the enemy?' Yes, he could fathom it, in a world so upside down, the living slept beneath the dead.

*

Helena liked him to pull her long hair over her head on the pillow and stroke her nape, to fall asleep to his touch there, like a cat, that soft little place, her dark hair flowing up, so thick there in his hand, fur, he thought, falling asleep watching Gillies' hand in the wet fur of a dog, everyone reeking. And now, beside her again, waking in the night thinking he was lying next to Gillies and dreaming of his wife.

*

Other women had refused to imagine the death of their husband, to refuse it any place in themselves; but Helena finally had learned that superstition was a form of irony that worked in reverse. If she faced it square, if she downed the possibility of it to the dregs, he would be spared. Immune. Isn't that how the new inoculation worked? By letting the poison inhabit her, she would keep him safe.

*

It took him some time to realise that the noises that woke him were in his head.

*

In the beginning, he believed he would not be like other men, he would never waste what was between them, he would remember everything. But he could not contain it all, their time already blurred. How long before it was all gone, before their years together were just a handful of images, sensations; how long before he would remember nothing?

*

Neither of them had siblings, Helena's parents were gone, there was no family to invite to their wedding; only his mother, and Helena's friend Ruth, from school-days. After the ceremony, they had tea at the church and then Ruth had to catch the train home. His mother took the train in the opposite direction. They spent their wedding night above the pub where they had met, in rooms kept for the rare traveller or a customer who'd had too much. It was a small room with a fireplace and a window next to the bed with a view of the fields. After closing time, that rural stillness. At last, when there was no sound left in the pub below and they thought even the proprietor would be in his bed, they undressed. She gave him a sophisticated silk dressing gown as a wedding gift. He gave her a brooch his mother had passed down to him for the occasion, a bird perched among notes on a musical stave, 'so there would always be harmony' between them. Missing her own mother, she cried, and pinned it to her nightgown, which sagged under its generous weight. From the window, they looked out to the place where they had stood that first night under the sky, at the gate of the station; before he lifted her nightgown over her head and saw her body in moonlight for the first time.

He did not expect to feel this, that he had become part of the human story, the countless who had lain together for the first time, who so easily might never have met, this magnitude they'd discovered that was only an emanation of blind chance – blind chance an argument for destiny he had never considered before.

*

When Helena slept, she looked just as she had their first nights together. As peaceful as moonlight across a field. He lay against her, hoping some of her peace would reach him. But instead, in the wasteland hours, her steady breathing made him feel cast out, forgotten, alone. He knew it should be enough, her resolute presence beside him, but sometimes he could barely restrain himself from shaking her so she must lie awake too. When sleep came at last, it was only another, more tortured form of being awake. Yet, she was still his. He slept for a while and, torn awake, woke her, to regain that little bit of sleep, and she never minded, was always his, wet fur, small stone. Sinking, buried.

*

Walking with his mother to the shops when he was young, streets silver after rain, swinging the empty basket, the basket that would be too heavy for him on the way home. His mother asked unanswerable questions, each a meditation, a desert cave, a mountain, a philosophical chasm to fall into; each the product of long pondering while going about the housework. Startling questions, a water bird puncturing the stillness of a lake from below, always making him wish he had an answer for her. 'Do you think we can really forgive someone if we don't know sin ourselves? Do you think that's the purpose of sin, to learn forgiveness?' She could have taken the raw material of her questions and made something comprehensive of them, if her education had been different, if she'd been given another sort of language, a different chance. He admired her intensely. He could say truthfully that his mother had never once hurt him, and he thought now of her infallible kindness with a sort of reverence, as something remarkable. Unerring.

*

His mother kept her list of questions in a diary beside her bed. How can two bodies make a soul? Why does the making of a soul have nothing to do with worthiness or otherwise? It was an argument for God he had never contemplated before.

*

You could put a word in front of your thoughts and see everything through that word – faith, family, war, illness. It could be your own word or someone else's, like wearing glasses that were the wrong prescription – wrong, or just not yours. Or, you could put your hands in front of your eyes in denial – but even so, he thought, you would continue to see, you can't stop seeing what's inside you. Everything that stakes its claim in us, everywhere that history stakes its claim in us. There are images that can, like certain rhythms, dismantle us, the way soldiers marching in step can take down a bridge. Maybe some images can take out parts of our brain, black them out, extinguish, obliterate parts of us. He continued to keep tally; if I can use words like extinguish and obliterate, then I am still intact.

*

The sea and the night sky had overturned and changed places; the whale swam across the sky, blacking out the stars. Unhurried as fate, a mesmerising, predatory slowness.

*

When I got back to your mother's, the house was gone.
   The rain fell through nothing, an empty place in the sky.
   He would not let her describe it. Each straining word in its inadequacy, a kind of lie. He needed words as uncompromising as numbers, the zero in an equation.

*

Disturbed chalk, glaciated chalk, chalk marl. The seam between England and France. *Caro et sanguis*. Flesh and blood.

*

After dinner, John went downstairs to develop the photograph of the young man, the young man's gift for his father. Was the son glad to be leaving his father behind? His own father had never begrudged him his chance in the world. He imagined this young man's father was so grateful his son had returned alive that he would be glad of anything, even if his son disappeared into a new life far away, even if he never saw his son again. This was a new world, with new degrees of grief, many more degrees in the scale of blessedness and torment. One leg lost, not both. One eye, one hand. But could one possibly ever believe, one son but not both?

He placed the negative in the developer and then into the fixer. The image in the fluid, like mist slowly parting the closer one approaches, began to emerge: the young man, beautifully clear and evocatively lit, handsome and whole in body; behind him, the luxurious drapery, the nap of velvet and details of brocade, sharp and precise; and in his hand, a book, Matthew Arnold's *Stanzas,* even the shadows of the letters embossed on the cover. And beside him, semi-opaque but perfectly distinct, an older woman, well dressed, pearl buttons, her fine head and lustrous hair, and her expression of intolerable longing.

*

The negative had been completely clean, John had placed the holder in the camera himself, he had taken the photograph himself, poured the developer himself. There was no possibility of tampering.

John investigated the image minutely.

He did not recognise the woman.

He searched the fixer with a single anguish of elation and disbelief, as if her image had been born of the fluid and had attached itself to the paper, as if there might be other images to be found in that clear liquid.

*

Some time later, John locked two prints in his desk in the studio. He wrapped the others for the young man and set them aside.

He left the lights off and went into the dark garden; a bit of moon, like a piece of bone dislodged, in the carbon black, the sound of the river. He walked to the beginning of the footpath, where no one could see him or hear him weep.

A sound startled him, the bushes shaking. It was Jip, with his darker fur across half his face, which made him look always, even in broad daylight, as if he were watching from the shadows.

*

It was still dark when John came back inside and returned to the studio. He looked again, in bright lamplight, at the woman's expression. Her love for the young man was electrifying, electrocuting. He rubbed at the paper as if the image could have been born even of the card. He had loaded the camera himself, the camera and plates were locked up at night – he never forgot to lock the cupboard, they were his livelihood – it was as reflexive as getting undressed every night. Would a man be sent a sign he could not understand? Wouldn't a spirit choose the exact way a man could know he was not being tricked? He was not credulous, he knew that our needs find their own methods, but no spectre had ever appeared to him in the trenches, no apparition, despite his need. Perhaps we are sent only exactly the kind of proof we can believe. Other manifestations would have been wasted on him, he would never have trusted visions in that hell – he knew about the Spectre of the Brocken and the Angels of Mons; he felt certain he would not have succumbed to belief. But here was indifferent evidence, extracted from machinery, chemicals, paper, and not even his own, but another man's ghost, proof separate and disinterested from his own desire. See, he could still think logically, he could still use words like disinterested, extracted, he was not deranged enough not to recognise these distinctions... He thought of the lucky charm almost every soldier kept – a stone, a snip of hair, a piece of coal, a wooden horseshoe, or a wooden pig the size of a thumbnail, trinkets from a fair.

Perhaps the exposure had come from his own body, his own hands; had it passed through him to the plate? Is that not what the human body is, is that not our own kind of photosynthesis – are we not chemistry that transforms light?

Celestographs, psychographs, Röntgen's electromagnetic waves, radiographs, X-rays. Was it not feasible, even probable? As scientifically accurate as electromagnetic waves, as X-rays? Were we not moving into an age where what is invisible to the naked eye is made visible through the eye of the machine?

Who can deny the reality of starlight? Yet the stars that give us their light do not exist. Who can say for certain that those who no longer exist, our dead, do not also reach us? And even those who do not believe, who live in a lead box of disbelief, must nonetheless accept – as the physicist Crookes proved in his experiment – that the electrical current we cannot see manifests itself on the plate in the lead-lined box, materialises in the dark of disbelief. From grief to belief.

In a long exposure, anyone who moves is invisible, only those who are still are perceivable.

It was like thermionic emission, a Fleming valve that allows transmission only in one direction.

He would write to Sir Ernest Rutherford, discoverer of the gamma ray and the proton; perhaps he would know the correct way to think about it, as something atomical, no less real than the world Sir Rutherford himself was mapping, the manifestation of the invisible. Who could say there are not bonds we had no knowledge of until now, until the technology gave us the means to see and understand? The camera sees more than the naked eye, grasps details that elude our perception, it supersedes our vision – every fibre of embroidery, every hair in a beard. Sometimes, surely, detects even thought. He would write to him. And only when he received an answer, no matter what that answer might be, would he tell Helena. If she were later hurt by his secrecy, he would say it was to protect her from fraud, from disappointment, from illusion; though of course she would know it was to protect himself from shame.

Yet he felt himself being carried out to sea, into belief, into vastness, and he could not bear to leave her behind.

He locked away the prints again. His leg was so painful he felt he might faint. He was barely able to climb the stairs. By the time he had unbuttoned his collar, he was asleep.

*

In the morning, he was still sleeping so deeply, so heavily, the first real rest since his return, that Helena could not bear to wake him. She made breakfast for herself, began mixing her paints for the first backdrop – spring – of the four seasons he'd asked for, and put the kettle on for a second time, only waking him at last when she heard Mr Stanley ringing the bell to be let in.

*

There are so many ways the dead show us they are with us. Sometimes they stay deliberately absent, in order to prove themselves by returning. Sometimes they stay close and then leave in order to prove they were with us. Sometimes they bring a stag to a graveyard, a cardinal to a fence, a song on the wireless as soon as you turn it on. Sometimes they bring a snowfall.

*

John saw the morning light at the edge of the curtains. He heard the bell ringing downstairs.

He wondered how it would feel to kneel at the side of the bed and pray. He wished his leg would let him kneel.

*

When John came downstairs, he saw that the sun was out and the street was shining from the rain, almost too bright to look at. He saw the patch of dampness at the doorway where Mr Stanley had shaken off his coat and cap and the trail of his wet shoes to the back of the studio. Mr Stanley was busy setting a scene – a basket of flowers, a garden wall, a waterfall, a parapet – and felt John's eyes on him and turned around.

'Everything alright?' asked Mr Stanley.

*

John brought out the photographs from the locked drawer. Even in his own excitement, he registered the satisfaction of seeing, for the first time, his assistant taken by surprise. Mr Stanley leaned over and scrutinised the image.

'I'm not sure I can be mixed up in anything like this, I'm sorry. I wouldn't have thought you were the sort. I'll take my wages now and be on my way. I won't say anything to anyone,' Mr Stanley added, 'not me to stick my neck into anything.' Then he paused. 'Expertly done, though, I'll give you that.'

'No, no,' John said, 'No. I swear to you.'

Together they went through the studio, meticulously checking the other plates, the equipment, the lock on the back door, which was intact – the tumbler lock and solid bolt jammed shut. Mr Stanley confirmed that every plate had been clean and loaded, untouched.

'What will you do?' Mr Stanley asked. 'Will you show him?'

'I don't know.'

'You must,' said Mr Stanley.

*

The young man arrived at midday.

'Are the photographs ready?' he asked.

'Yes.'

The young man reached into his pocket for his wallet.

'I think you should look first,' John said, 'to be sure they're satisfactory.'

John handed him the package and watched him unwrap it.

The young man's face was unreadable – John had never before witnessed such an expression. Beatitude.

'It's my mother,' the young man said.

*

Mr Stanley brought chairs and glasses and pulled a flask from his coat pocket, and they sat together in the back of the studio. They were suddenly blood brothers, a trinity, in shock.

The young man was shaking.

'We never said goodbye, she died when I was in Belgium. She's come to say goodbye.' He looked at them in challenge and alarm.

'Mother's love,' said Mr Stanley.

Was this any different than other strong feelings we know are real? We don't scorn the feeling of falling in love – why do we question other instincts, just as powerful, intangible, unprovable? Premonitions, a sensed presence, intuitions. Was this so different a faith?

'Are your parents alive?' the young man asked them.

John and Mr Stanley both shook their heads.

Mr Stanley turned to John. 'Did they die when you were a lad?'

'No.'

Silence. The smell of whisky. He couldn't believe he would tell them. Why not, then.

'An LZ, a baby killer,' John said. The Zeppelin that swam above his mother's bed and left a hole in the sky.

The young man understood at once. 'You came back and they were gone.'

'Just my mother.' John could barely speak. 'My father died when I was young.'

They drained their glasses. The young man looked at them, not knowing what to do. He stood and took out his wallet for a second time.

'No, no,' John said, feeling tears coming. 'I can't take money. It has nothing to do with me.'

'We can't take money for a miracle,' said Mr Stanley.

They tried to discuss the meaning of it, they had nothing to offer, they were silent, they were aghast.

The young man was going home to his father, he had a train to catch. When he was at the door, John called him back.

'You won't show anyone – promise me,' said John.

'I don't understand – it's miraculous – we must tell someone... The newspapers, the church!'

'Please.' He was beginning to raise his voice.

Mr Stanley intervened.

'Yes, wise to keep it to ourselves for now.'

'It might never happen again, we can't let people hope,' said John.

The young man looked at Mr Stanley, who paused, then nodded.

'Alright, sir. You know best.'

*

The young man left.

'May I speak my mind?' Mr Stanley asked.

John nodded.

'It's ungrateful. You could bear comfort. And if people pay, then you'll afford to help others, many others.'

'No.' He was agitated, sick. How could Mr Stanley think this could happen again? 'We could never take money! And you speak as though we could be sure of it – but it's grace.'

Mr Stanley looked at him meaningfully. 'We could be sure,' he said. 'Think of the lads who've come back, and all the ones who haven't. Sir. It would mean everything. You have a good reputation. People will believe you, believe in you.'

'No. And it's not me they should believe in.'

'Will you think about it? Give it serious thought?'

'Yes,' he said quietly, to be free of him. 'We'll close for the day – you may leave early – for a full day's wages.'

'Maybe you'll get some rest. Some time to think. Sir.'

*

Mr Stanley retrieved his cap and coat. John followed him to the door to lock up. He watched as his assistant crossed the road and, farther along, saw the young man at the corner, smoking. He saw Mr Stanley walk up to him, accept a cigarette. He watched as they walked down the road together.

*

'I saw you talking in the street yesterday. He did not catch his train?'

Mr Stanley replied without turning around.

'Oh aye, he was overwhelmed and decided to have another drink and catch a later train. I bought us a round.'

*

He struggled to sever yearning, to suffocate desire. Any expectation was despicable – ingratitude, for all he'd already received. It was deplorable, he was unworthy, wanting further proof. Yet, each time the clear, still pools of chemicals brought nothing more than the expected image, John felt a kind of alarm.

When he tried to open his mind to prayer, he found only perversion, disgusting memory, the render from the dead dripping onto his neck as he tried to sleep. No helmet to protect him from that anointing.

*

Then, developing the photograph of a young widow and her infant, a man emanated from the clear fluid, levitating above the young mother, half turned away, as if he had been caught weeping. When John showed the young woman the photograph, she staggered at the sight of her late husband, and they both looked at the dead man's face with terrifying elation.

*

When the third apparition materialised, it was a slight young man in uniform, barely in his twenties, hovering above a child, a robust boy in short trousers, whose picture they had taken that afternoon. He felt a shock of presentiment, that the soldier might be a fetch of the boy's future self. What did it mean, what messages was he bearing? It was torment not to understand the meaning of what he saw. This miraculous chemistry. The fact of being chosen, the task he had been returned for.

*

John watched Mr Stanley scrupulously putting everything away, making sure everything was in its place in the darkroom, cleaning every surface meticulously, as if wiping away fingerprints.

*

Finally, knowing it was too much, knowing it was gluttony, a blasphemy, he asked Mr Stanley to take his portrait. The nights he had wept next to his sleeping wife, ashamed of his hunger: the longing that his parents might come to him.

*

He knew many soldiers had kept a Bible in the chest pocket of their uniform. Consolation, he had assumed. But then it had been explained to him. The Bible is a very thick book, known to have stopped a bullet in an officer's pocket. A kind of solace after all.

*

The silence between Mr Stanley and himself was no longer an acceptance.

'You're selfish, sir. What's wrong with giving people hope?'

'That's right, you give hope, you don't sell it.'

'Forgive me, but that's not very clever. We could help so many.'

'No, Mr Stanley, I won't discuss it. Would you make money off the dead?'

He knew what Mr Stanley was thinking: the dead have no need of money. Sir.

*

Helena was in the garden bringing in tomatoes and lettuces for supper. She looked up at him as always, so open. John held her close so she would not see his face.

*

What is fate? When struggle is the same as surrender.

*

Desperate for sleep, he began to turn to Helena without tenderness. She gave herself; sometimes, gave in. Afterwards, a short sleep, too short, his only sleep, rescue at the last moment. Then awake again, hours to endure before daylight.

Even a month ago, Helena could not have believed he would ever lay his hands on her body and she would feel: here, and here, and here, he did not love her. She could not have believed that, in the world in all its mortal beauty, in the purple dusk above the trees, in the smell of their supper cooking, in this home they made together, in this kitchen, in this bed, here: he did not love her. Here and here on her body, all the places she had not owned in herself until he had named them, he no longer loved her.

If it is fact, he had once said of someone they knew, then it is not self-pity.

*

It was a day with three sittings: Miss Ames and her brother – library and drapery; Mr Scott and his wife – parapet and waterfall; Mrs Garnham and her four sisters – garden wall and a basket of flowers.

He came downstairs and found Mr Stanley already back from lunch.

'Just checking everything's in order,' Mr Stanley said.

He didn't take notice of Mr Stanley's expression until weeks later, waking suddenly in the night.

*

The next morning, Mr Stanley had again arrived early.

'How did you get in?' John asked.

'The door was unlocked when I arrived,' Mr Stanley said. 'I thought you'd opened it for me.'

They had been working together almost six months, it should please him, this assiduousness, yet it did not. They stood, two animals recognising each other in the forest. That was the worst of his perversion, John thought, the worst of his own sickness and suspicion – that it felt instinctive.

*

Helena stood in the doorway, as if calculating the distance the bottle on the table put between them. She thought she might cross the room and smash it in front of him. A long moment passed. She saw suddenly that it was complicity he wanted, no, corroboration, no, no more room for collaboration of any kind, no, a kind of coercion. Anything but to confide in her, to look her in the eye.

His leg stuck out in front of him, as if his trousers were nailed to a board. His hair, thick and greying, stood up in spikes, the hair she had once loved to grasp with both hands, knowing every atom of him. Even now, despite herself, she felt that no one else on this earth could be so kin.

She took a glass from the cupboard. She sat at the table and filled it to the brim, enough to make her sick.

*

When John told her at last, it was the middle of the night; he was talking before she was awake. His mouth against her ear, his voice so terrifying, someone else would have mistaken it for fury.

'Did Mr Rutherford answer you?'

'No,' he said. Pleading.

They lay so still, an accident of moonlight. To speak — a depth sounding, a detonation.

'John,' she said. He did not answer.

'Many times since she died,' Helena said, 'I've felt my mother with me. The night your mother died – how is it possible she left this earth without my feeling it? But now, I feel your mother too.'

We are born to face a single moment. She could barely hold him; skeletal, a bundle of sticks. She would let herself weep later.

'Sometimes,' she said, 'we don't understand something; instead – we know it. I held Ruth's son, moments after he was born, yet I cannot tell you what I saw. Suddenly he was present, not just bodily, but … where had he been before Ruth and Tom made him? He was suddenly entirely there, as if he had crossed from one state into another, like…steam to water, water to ice…'

She did not know what his silence signified. But soon he was sleeping quietly against her. The room was cold, she felt the heat of him. She imagined they had washed ashore in a new land.

*

John woke her gently so it would feel like part of her dreaming, and her response was instant, her welcome so immediate, her love overwhelmed him. He was inside the night sky and her cry seemed to be his own. They slept, a single dreamer.

He slept late, so late she was already in the kitchen. 'Thank the Lord for Sundays,' she said, as she always did; and he laughed, as he always had. And later she said, when they woke together a second time: 'It's always best to hear the church bells from bed…'

There was no seam of fear between them now, no seam between their bodies, no seam between him and the world, no seam between his mind and the blessing of sleep, no seam of disbelief.

*

When he photographed now, it was something miraculous: the light that bore witness onto the plate, the clear chemical light that saw and made visible something invisible. He felt everything in his subjects' faces, their fathomless sorrow and vulnerability as they sat motionless waiting for the light to seize their likeness. He felt the tiny buttons of the sitter's dress, the hands in the lap, the pale skin alive beneath their nervous restraint, every place on their bodies they had been touched or remained untouched, every place neglected, ignored, scorned, forgotten, shamed, adored.

*

How can we doubt the existence of what is invisible? How can we conflate invisibility with inexistence? Helena longed for a second soul in the darkness of her, growing into its name. Invisible, in the darkness of her. John. Or Anna. Anna, for his mother.

*

At last, apprehension came to him in his sleep.

His face was wet. Is it possible to weep in one's sleep?

He was instantly awake, more than awake.

No one would be sent a message he was unable to understand.

When he woke in the middle of the night, he knew that Mr Stanley had not served in the army at all.

*

He went downstairs.

There had been quite a lot of money in the drawer. He was beginning to panic. He looked at his watch, hours yet before dawn. He knew there would be no Mr Stanley arriving in the morning.

He saw that the plates and the spirit photographs were gone.

*

Helena woke alone; it was late, past the opening time for the studio; she hadn't heard him get up. She opened her eyes but didn't move, baking in the perfect warm place sleep had made. Sated, free, restored. When she went into the kitchen she saw a jar of wildflowers on the table.

*

He smelled the shadows in the garden, like sweating horses in the dark, the wet dog in the grass. He heard the broken voice of the river.

The moonlight – silver iodide. The photographic plate – a supernatural lake, waiting for a reflection.

Was that not what Alfred Russel Wallace himself had said – if we can appear in a photograph, then we must produce light.

*

The bedsheets were so white, it could be a coffin. Many times, he had prayed to die in a clean place. Would he know if he was dead?

Does the soul feel itself leave the body? Does it happen instantly? Will it hurt? Only if you have something to confess.

Mother, knit a prayer.

Each of his mother's questions a meditation, a desert cave, a mountain.

He had not been allowed to die to save her. The tears froze on his face.

But now, with the world white, he allowed himself to think of her. He drew her close and they lay together under the snow.

And Helena. He would die in the earth of her.

He opened his arms and she took her place next to him.

*

The water was so still. Had he crossed the weir?

He was no longer cold.

So still. When he looked down, he could see the stars.

*

He was found downstream, half out of the river against the weir, his eyes open. Unable to shut them, the under-taker gave him a blindfold, as if he were being readied for an execution.

*

In the middle of the night, Helena put a sweater over her nightgown and went into the garden. There she burned the backdrops she had painted, the perfect summer-lit path, the moonlit lake, the orchard full of birds. In the morning when she woke, she smelled the smoke in her hair before she opened her eyes. But she would not wash herself in water that came from that river.

*

All this time, he had forgotten this: after his father died, he had walked with his mother along the cliffs. A strong wind, the boulder-strewn margin of the sea. Suddenly they turned to each other. They had both smelled it distinctly — his father's tobacco. On the empty beach.

*

Sir Rutherford, I imagine an active surface where time and space meet, in constant excitation, time and space each igniting the other... We change space and we change time as we move — we cannot go back, instead we must move forward, into the past that exists as present memory, each movement altering the potential, each movement and thought changing the probability cloud of the future, 'the cloud of unknowing'. History is on one side of the equation, it can never be on both sides of the equation... A particle exists in space, a wave exists in time. Together they create a consciousness – consciousness itself the observer – and so the observed electron will always behave like both particle and wave, going forward into an ever-changing, single possibility... Why would it not be possible for the glass plate to capture what the eye cannot? ... I believe it is the plate that captures the image from the cloud of possibilities, drawn forth by our desire.

*

I slid the boat into the stars. You were waiting for me, at the edge of the trees, the bankside where morning comes first. It was as if you had always waited there, though I know it is not so. Sometimes you are there when the sky is just a little darker than the snow. I know you don't mean to startle me. It is my fault, suddenly remembering.

*

Gillies, who grasped the thick fur of a dog's neck to help him sleep.

*

His own hand clasping Helena's.

*

In its constant movement, even in its endless gradations of blackness, the night river was alive with light.

*

Like a candle flame, Helena had said, trying to erase an immense darkness.

*

In the flash of magnesium light, the frost on the fields – every crevice and serration, every stem and leaf – nothing invented, everything revealed. He saw every hair on Gillies' head, every eyelash and pore. The moon of Gillies' skull.

*

He saw now what he had missed. That, in the young man's photograph, the longing in the mother's face was beautiful. That it was the image of something true even in its corruption, despite its corruption. How could he have so misunderstood? Nothing, no desecration, no foulness and deception, could deny or erase that beauty, that longing.

*

'It's the voice of an angel, like the Miss Ella's, that should be the last voice we hear,' said Gillies.

John watched the nurses sitting at the bedside of the dying, each bed with its tiny lamp; it was some time before he realised he was looking at the night sky.

*

His mother's small sturdy black shoes.

The water felt quite warm now.

He turned to see Helena, asleep beside him.

No wonder he felt so warm.

*

It seemed to him now a very small correction; like the melting or freezing point, just a different cohesion, glassy or crystalline, gas or plasma. He is. He was.

III

RIVER WESTBOURNE, LONDON, 1951

What was the city to me? It was rain, narrow streets with lovers hiding in dark bedrooms opening their clothes to each other for the first time, the warmth, the shock, the gratitude. It was snow on the black roofs, the blush of light as it fades, lamps coming on across the square. The chairs carried out to the garden, the table too small for dinner, plates balanced on laps and left in the grass. Cafés, the smell of strong coffee and damp wool, the rain and wet snow on the floor of the mosaic foyer, the wooden door, the brass handle, thick white café crockery, cups that have touched so many lips, the friction match of desire — strike anywhere — no place on my body that was not ready to leap towards love, to be utterly consumed, to be owned and disintegrated, to rise out of that disintegration again and again, naked in our cold apartment, on the plank floor, the supper tray pressing against my waist, the mornings I went into the street feeling scoured and bare, free and strong with love, like a marble woman in a public garden, knowing you saw me naked in the street, at the crowded café tables, that there was nothing between your skin and mine, not in this entire city with its newspapers and doorways and shops and roofs white with snow and black trees and the hour of lamplight. It was as if I never wore a stitch of clothing for ten years, so owned and free was I in your touch and in your gaze, at every moment I could be yours and I lived for nothing else. One can work hard and listen to the news on the wireless and shout for what's right and fetch bread from the corner shop while the kettle is on, and still be clean and naked, new and untouched, ready to surrender all in a moment, the silk gathering between my legs as we ran up the stairs, the sound of my soft leather handbag falling to the floor inside the front door, the paper bag of groceries, the keys falling from your hand, ready to surrender all, ready to be struck to flame with a single touch.

*

Of course Helena knew who he was, browsing the shelves in his fine merino overcoat and paint-smeared trousers. The shopkeepers in the neighbourhood took it as a point of honour not to notice him, to ignore his celebrity as he picked his apples from their baskets, his bread and tea from their shelves, finally reaching into his pocket and searching for loose change, when everyone knew his handwritten shopping list could have been sold to buy a house.

She did not understand for some time why he had plucked her — middle-aged, a pear turning soft in the bowl — from the bookshop. At first, she thought it was because of what she'd been reading behind the counter — Mr Ayles never objected to his staff reading once the chores were done. And then she thought it was because he had identified her as a specimen of a particular kind, a woman who, for one last moment, was still able to be wounded in that one way; who might, with a single touch, be brought back to life exactly once more. She was convinced it was this gratitude in particular — ignited by his pity — that he could never have enough of, one source of the great flow of gratitude his presence seemed to arouse in everyone.

That evening, Mr Graham Rhys, figurativist, had come in from the rain, in his stained trousers and expensive coat, a paper parcel under his arm and hair dripping; he was counting out change for a used Penguin when he looked up and saw her for the first time, though he had often been in the shop before, paid and never bothered to look her in the face. For a moment, he seemed to take in what she was — she gave him that — his look like the lamps of a freight train bearing down on a field at night, a huge glaring light that suddenly floods everything in range — and then he hesitated, turned away and left, the shop suddenly in darkness again. The only other customer, a young man standing in Fiction who had been watching from the corner of his eye (for of course the painter had been recognised), went back to browsing the shelves, while Helena stood, unable to move from behind the counter, looking at the door, knowing something had just occurred and not knowing what it meant; as if his future had somehow intercepted hers, jostling it out of place, just enough to swerve her off course, the single centimetre one way or another that saves one or sets one in the path of an oncoming car. Soon after, it was time to close the shop, walk home, see if her daughter had called, heat the soup in the pot, and climb into bed, eager for another day to be behind her. That night, she dared to look down at her body – something she never did unless fully clothed – and saw she was still quite trim, still strong enough; just a glance, as one might glance to check if there was enough milk left in the fridge for tea in the morning, and nothing to be done about it at this hour if there was not.

*

'I will only pay you if you are prompt and if you do exactly as I say.'

She nodded.

'Do you mind?' He squeezed her arm, her belly. 'For a few inches of flesh, you are ashamed. So much loneliness just because of a pinch of skin.'

He was so earnest in his observation, as if he were doing her a kindness, that it felt ignoble to reply that no part of her body felt extra at all.

Helena soon learned that he never lied in detail, but in essence; and so, she felt free to lie in detail but not in essence, believing his falseness to be, by far, the greater.

Mr Rhys offered a good price, more money for one night than Helena earned in a week, so she agreed to pose for him, giving herself entirely to the discomfort between them.

*

At 2 a.m., sitting by the fireplace melting cheese over scraps of bread with nothing but a blanket to hide her sixty-year-old body, scrutinised by a stranger who had hardly spoken a word all evening. Perhaps this is not everyone's idea of paradise. On the bare plank floor, the oil from the cheese dripping down her fingers as she crammed the bread into her mouth, the first night in all her life that her daughter would not have known where to find her.

*

After a few days, she began to bring groceries, one satchel's worth – bread, cheese, fruit. A jar of soup and a saucepan. Two spoons.

'I don't live here,' he said, 'there's another place around the corner. Where the spoons are. But thank you for bringing them, all the same. And this soup! It tastes like the earth of Tuscany.'

'It's the celery,' she said, 'sliced very thin.'

'Thin as a fingernail,' he said. With approval.

*

'Talk to me, tell me about your life.'

'I've had a lot of lives,' she lied. 'It could take some time.'

She wondered if he cared at all what she was saying, whether he was even listening. Whether he wanted her to talk only so he could see how her mouth and jaw and neck moved. The rest of her, the flesh that had grown a soul inside it – suddenly her love for her daughter made her care for it, how could she be so disrespectful of the body that had made her dearest Anna? And she could see that he thought it was his looking at her that had done this – as soon as she knew it, as soon as her thoughts and feelings had changed, he noticed. And she was so angry that she fought hard not to weep. *To acknowledge one's own pain is not self-pity.*

*

'You might have remarried, you still look good.'

'What for?'

He laughed. It was interesting, making him laugh.

'Remarriage would have interfered with my career,' she said, 'as an ill-paid shop-girl.'

'What was your husband's name?'

'None of your business.'

He laughed again. She was beginning to feel entertained herself.

'What did you do before you worked at the bookshop?' he asked.

'I was a fencer. I taught stage-fighting.'

'Tell me about fencing,' he said.

'I gave it up.'

'Is that when you became an ill-paid drudge?'

'No.'

'What did you do after you were a fencer?'

'I was a mime.'

'I take it you won't tell me if you have children,' he said.

'No, I won't.'

'I have five children,' he said, 'with three different women. I've been married once and the other women I never lived with.'

'You say it as if it had nothing to do with you.'

'Three girls and two boys,' he said.

'You mean, three daughters and two sons.'

He paused. 'Yes.'

'Why do you want me to take my clothes off if you're only going to paint my face?' she asked, though she knew the answer. To make her vulnerable, subordinate, guarded.

'Bodies are not very interesting. Variations of the same. Flesh hanging off the bone. It's ironic that it's our face we expose – the most personal part of us. We think we remember or recognise a face, but a face is always different.'

That was his signature comment, she'd read it in magazines more than once.

'You didn't answer my question.'

'Because it makes you want to hide something else, and that shows up in your face. And then I have to discover what that is,' he said.

'It amuses you.'

'It interests me.'

'What if I want to put my clothes back on?'

'Then I'll be a bit angry, because we had an agreement and I've already begun. But I'll still pay you for the rest of the day and we'll say goodbye.'

She considered the fact that this was the only time she had taken off her clothes for a man in almost three decades, that her body had nothing really to do with her anymore, that she could put the money away for the train fare to visit Anna.

'I'll keep my word,' she said.

'I'm glad.'

And she realised he had just taken the measure of her thoughts in her face while she hadn't noticed.

'When my children were at university,' she lied, 'I became an apprentice in a bakery. All those years crawling out of bed at the sound of the alarm, making sure they were ready for school, the book bags packed, the lunches, the handkerchiefs, the shoes in the satchel when it rained. So many mornings I thought I couldn't wait for a time when I could finally sleep in, have my waking thoughts to myself, and then, when they were gone, I was still wide awake at dawn, and leaping out of bed to avoid dread, despair, uselessness. So, I began to work at the local bakery, what could be better at 4 a.m. than setting out the pans, learning to use the great mixing machines?'

'Was that before you took the job at the bookshop?'

'Yes, long before. In between I was a horse breeder, a shorthand teacher and an announcer for the railways.'

'Because of your stentorian voice.'

'No.'

*

Anna had accepted a job in a hospital a five hours' drive away. They agreed that Helena would remain until Anna knew if she liked it — if it was a mistake, she could come home. It made sense not to give up the flat yet, and her job, until Anna was sure she wanted to stay.

They spoke once a week, usually before supper. Helena heard about Anna's landlady, the head of the department, her colleagues. Soon Anna made friends and was not always home for supper and instead they would talk before sleep, hundreds of miles apart. Before hanging up, Anna would plan when they'd talk next time, at supper or bedtime. The dear minutes. Goodnight darling, goodnight Mama, goodnight, goodnight.

And then the long insomniac night, reading entire books borrowed from the shop and returned the next morning. The hateful sight of the clock — 3 a.m., 4 a.m. The scalding nightmare. Reading in bed is a precision art — knowing the right wattage, high enough to read by, low enough to fall asleep with the light still on, choosing books not for their content but for their size and weight, knowing the right position in bed so the book won't slide off and hit the floor and wake you again.

*

We woke to a morning of mid-winter fog. From the window above our bed, we saw that the surrounding buildings had disappeared.

'The mountains are shrouded in mist——'

'It will be at least two weeks before the rescue party arrives—'

'We'll have to live on human flesh—'

'And use body heat to keep warm…'

Sometimes you would close the studio early and slip upstairs to find me.

Find me, John.

There is a garden in a suburb of Paris I have never seen. A square wooden table and wrought-iron chairs weathered by decades, lilies bending in the rain. In our bed, you described this garden; for some reason, I wept. It was a place enravishingly familiar, as if I had known it long ago and had held it, always, close in memory. Then I thought it might be a future memory, something awaiting us. But I did not know then it was our last afternoon. The window was open and we could hear the trees.

Places described by a lover are like no other places on earth. To learn a city in this way — boulevards curving, canals, cornices overhead — in the naked embrace, the luxury of listening while your skin is listening. The city slips into your body. And then, if you are fortunate enough to arrive there for the first time with that same lover, or more fortunate still to arrive there after many years with the same lover — then you will enter the place as if in a dream. Your body will recognise the canals, the cornices, the curving boulevards; memory before sight. And that is a great gift, because we arrive most often as strangers; this, of course, is its own pleasure. But this other pleasure — arrival into the memory of a place you've never been and yet know in *your skin — is the same as arriving into love, that knowledge of something we do not yet know. The kind of love that is like a fatality. The one you never live beyond, no matter what else befalls you.*

*

'You may as well put your clothes on,' he said. 'What would it take to see you naked?'

A ghost, amnesia, a grandchild.

She suddenly felt she wanted him to know her. How utterly necessary it became, for just one moment, to be known by him.

'Maybe if we painted each other,' she said.

She was shocked at how ravenous she was, feeling the brush in her hands. At first, for him, it was a lark. But soon enough, it was not.

'When did you learn to paint like that?' he asked.

'During the first war.'

'You work in a shop – do you paint at night?'

'I haven't held a brush in thirty years.'

He was suspicious of her now. The sight of her at the easel no longer amused him. So, the next day, instead of picking up the brush, she again took off her clothes. But whatever strange contract had been between them was broken.

When she arrived the day after, there was another woman in the studio. Very young. That was the first moment she understood her work might be good.

That night, she was glad Anna could not see her tears as she pressed the phone to her ear, aching to her daughter's dear voice. She was calmed by Anna's stories of her day and the thought of her making supper, even in her kitchen so far away. Helena began to draw on the message pad by the phone. She did not realise what she was doing until John's face was looking back at her, as if he had risen from the paper, she thought, as if he had been imprisoned there and now was free.

'What are you making tonight?'

'Oh, just a scramble,' said Anna, 'with onions and parsley. And for after, the biggest roundest orange you've ever seen in your life.'

I will paint that orange, which I can't see but only imagine, I will paint it bigger than a Zurbarán and bring it to our Anna. And then it will not matter if I ever paint again.

IV

RIVER ORWELL, SUFFOLK, 1984

At the back of the shop, Peter sat at a large table, the Anglepoise leaning over him, as if searching for errors in his work. He heard the front door open, with its bell on a hinge, and a voice call out:

'On Amsterdam Island, it's 4:01 p.m.; in Perth, it's 11:01 p.m.; in Alert, it's 10:01 a.m.!'

He looked up. Thank God. She was home.

*

He held her. She was long, like a pine marten, a single pure muscle.

All in one piece. Thank God.

*

Peter closed the shop. They went upstairs. He did not want her to know how much he'd missed her. Whenever Mara was away – saturated, silted with fear for her. Unbearable.

'I missed you,' Mara said. 'Miss me?'

His tears seeping out.

She held him, squeezed the life into him.

'Dad,' she said, 'Dad. Don't worry, I'm staying.'

He wept like a child.

*

She brought out the griddle.

They ate pancakes for supper because it was a tradition between them when she came home and because she liked the glass bottle of maple syrup with its tiny, useless handle.

He watched her eat, filling her hollow leg. Nineteen pancakes. He made them small. But still. Starving.

He was beginning to come back to life.

'In Madrid, it's 3:49 p.m.,' he said. 'In Mauritius, it's 6:49 p.m.'

He would do anything for the sight of that lopsided grin.

*

He joined her on the sofa where she was reading — when she came home, always one of her mother's books, with her mother's name, Anna, carefully written on the inside cover, and the date and city where Anna had bought it — *Jane Eyre*, *The Horse's Mouth*, *Portrait of the Artist as a Young Man* — the bindings gone completely soft, re-read countless times — to prove to herself she was home again. He sat beside her and she put her feet in her thick woollen socks on his lap the way she always did.

'When Alan comes, would you wear the beautiful kilt Grandmum gave you?' she asked. 'We have a bet. He doesn't believe you'll wear it. If you do, he has to buy us all dinner at Moro's.'

'Ha! We'll show him then. I'll even wash behind my knees.'

The room was lamplit, warm. Mara had made a sturdy fire, she had always been good at that — a point of pride. She continued to read and he was almost asleep when Peter heard her say, 'I missed her more than ever this time. Everywhere we were made me think of her, I almost thought I'd see her if I turned my head.'

He was fully awake now.

'Sometimes I think I see her too,' Peter said, 'out of the corner of my eye. If you can see a feeling.'

'Yes, I think you can.'

*

Peter had learned his trade from his father, who was himself the son of the best tailor in Piedmont. In the end, Peter's father had found he preferred his uncle's trade and became a hat maker. Then grandfather and father worked together, outfitting – 'from the top of the head to the soles of the socks' – gentlemen from Liguria, Lombardy, Emilia-Romagna, his father even covered the heads of gentlemen from Switzerland and France. He also designed women's hats, to please his wife, Lia, Peter's mother. His grandfather found them a business partner and they made uniforms and hats for the military. When war came, they were suddenly wealthy. Uniforms had been his grandfather's idea, and when his grandfather and both Peter's parents had died, Peter inherited their part of the business, sold their share and crossed the Channel. In London, he and Anna were standing next to each other in a queue for a Marian Anderson concert and a week later they discovered themselves sitting a row apart listening to Myra Hess. One of the first things he learned about Anna was that she was an admirer of Eglantyne Jebb. Anna, who had served in field hospitals in France, had just accepted a new job in a hospital in the north and was celebrating before leaving London. A few months later, with all her letters in his coat pocket, Peter took the train north and Anna took him home.

Peter had money, but he was not proud of it and he did not want to stop working. He opened a small workshop – surprisingly, men never seemed to stop wearing hats – and he and Anna, newly married, lived above it.

They did not want much, and they lived on what they earned, leaving the money from his family's business mostly untouched. It was to be their nest egg, their daughter Mara's inheritance. Peter did not have any inclination to live another kind of life. Anna was in agreement, and she had the freedom to go where she was needed.

*

Peter and Mara had a game they played when Anna was away. At first, he had shown Mara the map to soothe her, to make her believe the world was not so large, that her Mama was not so far. 'Look – she's here – just a few inches away!' She would touch his finger as he pointed, then touch the place with her own finger, then take her father's big face in her tiny hands.

'Can we telephone?'

'Not yet – where Mama is, it's three o'clock and she's at work.'

It took some explaining, but eventually Mara understood: when it was morning where she was, it was afternoon where her Mama was. When she ate her dinner, her mother was going to sleep. Soon Mara knew the time zones and could measure her ache for her mother with pinpoint accuracy.

*

When Mara was young, she conquered the sewing machine with the natural talent of a draughtsman with a pencil, as adept as the great-grandfather she'd never known. If she saw an apron or a tea towel she liked, she made a skirt; she saved scraps and in twenty minutes was dressed for the opera. Her secret was being unafraid to go freehand, never measuring. Measuring made her nervous, slowed her down. Mara was resourceful, she trusted herself. He knew that was one of the reasons they always asked for her, and one of the reasons she always went. He still joked that if she could, she would carry her sewing machine in her backpack. Maybe, he joked, she came home because she missed her sewing machine. Now, between fork-fuls of pancake, she told him she would feel blessed to be able to work in a clinic or an emergency ward. It only took a moment for him to understand. It was a man. She was in love. He never thought he'd be grateful to lose her that way. But someone else had brought her home and Peter was already half-mad with gratitude.

*

Her lover was a journalist. As Peter watched his daughter devouring pancakes at the kitchen table, he imagined that Mara had met her man in the hospital, that she had repaired him, that Alan had come out of the anaesthetic and seen her eyes full of kindness. That he had watched her move through the ward, seen how she listened, how she held the gaze or the hand of the shattered men she examined with such gentleness, while she assessed, absorbed information with uncompromised efficiency. That he was fascinated, awestruck. Peter imagined the scene, like cinema.

'Where shall we live?'

'I need to be near my father.'

'Then that's where we'll be.'

He knew Mara had always thought love made things complicated, but Peter knew love was a sharp blade slicing an apple: cleaved – both blade and bond.

*

Mara had been away for weeks, trucked from place to place, boarded wherever there was room, waiting overnight in pick-up locations. The permanent lack of sleep in any other circumstance would have felt like an illness; now it was continuous proof she was still alive.

In the ruins, the smoke chafed the back of her throat, but it was dry and quiet and she slept like a stone. When she woke, she saw him sleeping next to her. Later Alan would tell the story of how he had found her. But she would never forget the feeling that she had found him, simply by opening her eyes.

*

After he was flown out, she sobbed for two days. Then she felt scoured; the boulder inside her chest was gone. It had been replaced by emptiness. That was better.

*

When he returned home, Alan wrapped the strap around his camera, put it in the bottom of his rucksack and locked the rucksack in a suitcase. He would have thrown the suitcase in the river if he'd had the energy to carry it there. Then he locked himself up too, to seal off his contagion.

There was no one to care if he slept all day. He lived on terrible takeaway from the place on the corner, because they were willing to walk the few steps and leave it at his door, each greasy bag miraculous. He knew the moment would come when he would be ready to start again and, until then, he would sink like a frozen toad in its stinking hibernaculum, heart slowed almost to death, hardly needing any oxygen, letting everything he had witnessed rot in him. It was self-pity and a reeking indulgence but he didn't care. It was what he needed, he was used to it now. But, he thought, this time, it might truly be the last.

He locked himself in and lay there, until he was absolutely certain he could not live without her.

He wondered if he would be able to hope in the total and depthless way necessary to make it work, to not let go. He knew he must not let go. Not her.

One November morning, almost two months after his return, Alan walked to the end of his street and posted the letter. He noticed the blotting-paper sky absorbing the dusk, the bronze leaves soaked and shining, half-bare branches in the wind. He was wearing his father's sweater. It smelled as it always did, of oiled wool and cedar-scented aftershave. He was not quite warm enough but was glad of the cold.

His father had been a compact man, always tidy and contained. But unashamed to express his love, and to cry when necessary. He had witnessed his father cry three times. After Alan's mother's funeral, when Alan had left for his first war and when Alan had returned that first time. It seemed long ago.

He pushed the letter, irretrievable, his single chance, into the dark chasm of the post box. Irrevocable, he thought, as a grave. He did it quickly, as if he were throwing away all the hope left in the world.

*

Peter knew it was his fault as much as Anna's that their daughter chose refugee camps, field hospitals, the most dangerous places. His obsession, injustice, bloody Marx, bloody Gramsci. He should have raised her to selfishness.

Mara had her mother's bravery.

'I need to go where I'm needed most — otherwise, what's the point?' Mara said.

Stay where you're needed most. Stay.

'Where's Mama?'

Mara's small legs swinging over the edge of a kitchen chair, a summer Saturday morning, the back door open, the hose filling the paddling pool with water. Peter fetched the map.

'She's there,' he said, using Mara's finger to point. Where the sky is burning.

*

It sickened Alan to report, to analyse, from a distance. But he knew, like a dog that smells an earthquake coming, that if he went back one more time, he would die there.

When neighbourhoods were bombed into oblivion, when entire worlds vanished — the living network of shops, schools, street life, families, and the organisation of systems and memories in a single body and soul – Alan knew that everything he wrote was from knowledge so inadequate, so liminal, it was like describing the complexity of a molecule from the vantage point of the moon. He was less than a messenger, less than a clerk with his accounting book, not even a transcriber. He despised the term investigative journalist and could never feel comfortable among the posse. He was feral, pretended nothing, something mongrel, a renegade who made his own raids on places, dashing in and out and trying to write at least like a human camera. He got into trouble. He kept his nerve, until he lost it. And there, in his useless state, he found her, asleep. Mara had disappeared into the street, exactly the wrong thing to do, but some instinct, Alan thought, had saved her, the hospital bombed while she was between point B and point A, on her way back from seeing a patient because a mother had begged her. 'No mother,' she told Alan, 'should ever need to beg for her child's life, and never, never should she need to beg to me.' There was military planning, there were raids, there were administrative rules and there was chaos. Mara had taken her one chance, there is always only one. And Alan had met her in the middle of his own chance and had fallen asleep some distance from her, as if they were sharing a refuge.

*

They talked for the first time, lying in the splintered dust. Alan knew he would soon be going home.

'Do you think it will ever be possible,' Mara asked, 'for an hour to go by and not to want to put your fist through a wall or scream at people to open their eyes?'

'No,' he said.

They lay next to each other in the dimness. He imagined them on two gurneys awaiting transfusions.

It was different, thinking about her misery, her rage, instead of his own.

'Maybe,' he said.

*

Mara had lit the fire. She had baked a cake, and a slow stew was simmering under a lid of pastry.

They ate with pleasure. Alan fell in with them, it had been easy.

Then she piled the dishes in the small sink and whatever dishes would not fit remained on the table.

Afterwards, with her father sitting on the other end of the sofa and Alan in the large faded upholstered chair, they read aloud. Because Alan had said to her, 'Do what you always do. Please, just let me in.' She liked books that seemed to begin again at the middle, the way life so often did, the way a day or an evening or a conversation or a song or a long, worthwhile idea so often did. The way love so often did.

When it was her father's turn to read, he chose Rilke. 'Every angel is terrifying...'

Mara had not intended to bear witness, and she did not know if she did so in order to challenge the safety of being home, or to make that safety more real. She had thought her father desperate not to know, not to let it into the haven he'd made for them. But she also knew that her mother must have told him everything; so that when Anna returned, Peter would not be more alone. It had not been selfish of her mother to speak, but the opposite; speaking was unbearable. Piercing the skin to release the infection. It was Alan's presence that made Mara speak now; that made her want to prove to her father that, even with Alan with them, she would never leave him.

She told them about her friend, a nurse who had more experience and compassion in her hands than Mara felt she would ever have, who had taught Mara to break the impossibly strong suction force trapping a child's head by simply inserting her finger at the edge of the womb, a nurse whose own children lived too far away to visit, the same nurse who had ridden a bicycle through the dark, no light to give her away, packets of medicine taped to her skin under her waistband, who plummeted into an abyss that had not been there only hours before on the only road out, the medicine looted, her body looted, thrown away. Mara told them of surgery by electric torch, held by the patient's mother. Children too young to give birth. Doctors turned to ice with emotion. The nurse who fell asleep in the middle of an operation. The infant put back together after hours of surgery, only to be killed by a bomb that fell on the hospital a moment later. The father who kept a scrap of cloth tied with a string around his neck, filled with teeth, proof his son had existed, though Mara knew he would never be sure they were his son's. The same man who watched his shoes being stolen from his feet by someone who thought he was dead. What she told them was scalding smoke from the fire, with the rest still unsaid, burning her mouth, impossible yet to say.

Every present eternal minute, alert to the meticulous order and detail of a human body, in defiance of what had been done to it, and alert to her own convulsive rage. Her father heard everything she said, Mara knew it. And Alan's eyes, which had seen just as much, had never left her face. It did not matter if what she said was too emotionally expressed, or told with the voice of an automaton. What mattered was beginning to speak aloud what she had hoped she would never have to tell, and that she had been received and understood. It mattered like Alan's sleeping breath on her skin.

And when she told them of the deer that had come into the graveyard as if to read the gravestones, the gravestones that were all that was left of the burnt village, and the water bird emerging so close it pierced the reflection of the boat, when she told them she was absolutely certain of her mother's presence at those moments, in those places of torment and abandonment, it was so they would know that Anna had never stopped teaching her, how to give her life and give up her life, how to measure friendship in extremity and, mother and child, systole and diastole, how to love when you have nothing left.

*

In Mara's experience, the supernatural was purely the presence of good, the love that burns free of the corpse; always love that tries to escape the human terror.

*

Everywhere the dead are leaving a sign. We feel the shadow but cannot see what casts the shadow. The door opens in the hillside, in the field, at the sea's edge, between the trees at dusk, in the small city garden, in a café, in a tram in the rain, on a stairway.

*

It was late now, so late, time for Alan to return to the hotel. Mara embraced her father before he went up to bed. She felt how bony and stiff he was, under his beautiful, worn tweed jacket. But she would not think of him as old, she would not let this sadden her, not tonight. And when she and Alan walked out together into the dark garden, the fox was so still they did not see it at first, still as a resin figure on a lawn. He squeezed her arm and pointed, actually pointed, like in a movie or a painting, too astonished even to say the word: look.

*

Alan called her when he got back to his hotel, not far from where she lived with her father.

'Are we real?' he asked.

'Yes,' she said.

'Are you still there?'

'I'm trying to go to sleep.' She laughed.

'May I come back right now?' he asked.

'Yes,' she said.

She was waiting for him at the front door, so he wouldn't knock and wake her father. She was wearing a nightshirt, a long T-shirt with the faded image of a cartoon dog on it. 'I've had it since I was a teenager,' she said. 'I wear it to prove to myself when I wake in the night that I'm really home.'

They squeezed into her single bed.

'Tell me everything,' he said. 'Where were you happiest? What was your favourite food when you were a child? What was the first book that made you cry? I want to hear everything, don't leave out a thing.'

'That will take forever,' she said.

'I hope so.'

*

Alan came for dinner again the following night: shepherd's pie, greens, a chocolate Bundt.

*

Alan stayed. He found an apartment nearby; soon she was living there too.

'My father has a present for you,' said Mara.

'I've made you a cap,' Peter told Alan. 'My judgement of head circumference is usually excellent, but if it doesn't fit perfectly, I can easily fix it. I was going to use thornproof tweed because it's incredibly strong and forgiving – if it's punctured you can work it with your fingers and the wound will usually close.

But because of its history — the first thornproof was worn by the Canadian militia in 1870 — the Red River Rebellion — I've chosen a measure of this beautiful ancient weave from South Uist that I've had on hand for many years. This cap will keep you warm, it will keep off the rain and snow. It's good for waving from the deck of a boat, or fanning a fire. Depending on the landscape, it's camouflage.'

This cap, crushable without harm in a pocket, woven by hand, measured and cut and sewn by hand, Mara's father's hand. More protection than a steel helmet.

Alan saw the colours of the tweed: winter sky, moss, travertine, mountains. He thought of places he would take Mara to, as if those places belonged to him. It was an aching with all the loneliness he'd known and all the gratitude he felt now.

*

Mara and Alan walked home through the winter streets. Past midnight, hardly any lights in the windows, the night sky deepened by the clarity of the cold. The snow-fall began so gently it could only be seen under the streetlamps. Silent, lambent emanation.

'I understand why you don't ever want to leave him,' Alan said.

Mara took his hand.

'I'm sleeping in this cap tonight,' he said.

The next morning, he came to breakfast wearing it.

'I'm never taking it off,' he said.

*

At the big table under the Anglepoise lamp, Peter imagined his daughter and her lover crossing the luminous city as the snow fell. The refuge of their small apartment. His heart ached, remembering.

*

'Do you think it's possible,' Mara asked, 'for good to survive long enough, to outlast, to wait, to endure, while evil consumes itself?'

It was a philosopher's question, a parent's question, a lover's question. Was it a doctor's question? Alan wasn't sure.

'No,' he said.

He knew no one could get in or out now. She knew it too. It was a secret between them, that they both knew the same failure, that even if they could go back, there or elsewhere, they would not last a day. It would be a kind of suicide; they were no longer ice cold. Would it always feel like failure?

They lay beside each other in the dark. Alan knew
with all his soul that he loved her.

'Maybe,' he said.

V

RIVER ORWELL, SUFFOLK, 1964

Anna felt the air change abruptly, felt a whirring, like the rubber blades of a fan, she felt buzzed by an invisible obstruction. Saturday morning, no one home, where was Mara – not in her bed. The house so quiet, Mara's cardboard village made of cereal boxes and shoe boxes painted happy colours, arranged across the floor, paper and paintbrushes on the kitchen table – perhaps they had just dashed to the shop for something, strange they hadn't let her know. They had never not been home to greet her, Mara rushing into her arms. Anna looked out into the garden, the paddling pool filled with water; they couldn't have gone far, surely wouldn't be gone long. The floor by the back door was wet, Mara's pink sandals. How strange, the sound of Mara's voice and, flashing in the sunlight, shining mid-air, the water in the pool splashing by itself.

VI

RIVER ORWELL, SUFFOLK, 1984

They could have been in a forest hut on the rim of a fjord, or in captain's quarters on a galleon, those first weeks together, evenings by the fire with Mara and her father, talking of Mara's mother, Anna, and of Mara's childhood and her summer with her grandmother in Flamborough Head, her father's boyhood in Piedmont, Alan's nine lives. For the first time in his life, Alan had the experience of not avoiding haunted ground. Candour; ardour; on the old sofa amid cushions and blankets that had been well worn by thousands of afternoons and evenings spent next to the fire reading, and amid an accumulation of detail he, like an archaeologist in a newly discovered settlement, could not get enough of – the books, the charity shop finds and souvenirs, the fire screen that looked scavenged from a medieval junkyard, corduroy, crochet, stones brought home from wild places, the abstract painting that turned his heart to yearning, in colours of winter dusk or the sea, signed by someone named Sandor, who had also painted Mara's mother, her long hair, huge sweater hiding her hands to her fingertips, her face — Mara's face — solemn, luminous with love. And a painting by Mara's grandmother: an orange so lavish and heavy it toppled out of the frame into the room, like a boulder, an avalanche of pleasure. Alan had always thought it impossible for words to fully witness and describe what the world was. But now, for the first time, being with Peter and Mara, in their house with them, he felt it impossible to describe what the world might be.

They had made their encampment, the three of them, just like that, as if Alan had always been meant to arrive at their door, a stranger; he could not have formulated his need for this shelter in all its idiosyncratic exactitude and yet, in the broken world of generosity and dispossession, bereavement and blind luck, without any credit in the bank of belief, he had been found by them.

*

Slowly Alan saw proof accumulating, in his and Mara's own small apartment, of their weeks and months together: knowing he would find her shoes under a certain chair, her handbag and scarf in a corner of the kitchen, the book of nineteenth-century Russian set design found in a church sale propping open a door.

He loved their aimless drives and the joy of return. He loved their walks together to settle the day, dusk into dark, making their meal together, the quiet mending that comes of speaking and listening, sometimes a surprise for dessert in its little bakery box; the feel of her in his arms as they listened to music, read aloud. Above all, shared desire, with its unfathomable, inexpressible peace. The hope implicit in their days and nights together.

*

To the historian, every battlefield is different; to the philosopher, every battlefield is the same. War has ever redefined the battlefield; we no longer pretend to fight on designated ground, instead recognise the essential substratum where war has always been fought: exactly where we live, exactly where we have always believed we were sheltered, even sacredly so, the places we sleep and wake, feed ourselves, love each other – the apartment block, the school, the nursing home – citizens ingesting the blast and instantly cast in micronised concrete, rigid as ancient Pompeiians in volcanic ash. Snipers, barrel bombs. The strategic bombing of hospitals, to prove how senseless it is to save lives in a war zone, senseless as stopping up a hole in the hull of a ship at the bottom of the sea. What history is war writing in our bodies now? War fought by citizens whose muscles have never before held a gun or passed a child overhead, hand to hand, to a mother in a train car crammed immobile with refugees. The war being written in these bodies, in this child's body, will be read as war has always been read: stranger to stranger, parent to child, lover to lover. And, even if it is possible to return to one's city, even if one has never left, it will be a history told as it has always been told: far from home.

What was Alan's task? To write what no one could bear to read. What was anyone's task? To endure the truth. To act upon it. But even empathy, compassion, was to feel and think in terms of separation. And Alan could only feel and think now in terms of entirety, of humanity as a single organism, a single entity of cause and consequence, the human union of breathing and being we are born to. A man's brain spraying across your face. A baby in the womb, a bullet hole in its forehead. Exsanguination. Decapitation. The physics of ballistics in human bone and tissue. Soldiers praying for a successful massacre.

*

Alan was haunted by endlessly divisible degrees of failure; everything he did or thought, inadmissible – his failure itself a privilege. Believing every word made a difference and knowing nothing he said made a difference. Did the truth matter sometimes? No, it mattered or it didn't.

The fight for necessities – water, food, shelter, schools, hospitals, a common good. As always, he would take his tipper lorry of language and empty the horror in plain view, so no one could claim they had not known. There was nothing more to say and, of course, he would go on saying that same nothing.

*

Only Alan, Mara thought, understood her fury at the obscenity of the shops, aisles of abundance like temple offerings for the gods; at her colleagues' impassioned debates about the merits of certain restaurants as if they were moral questions. She could not adjust the levels in herself, the speed and volume inside, her ever-greater foreboding and rage. She could not acclimatise to the hospital's reliable electricity, ready machinery, shifts that ended, the safe walk home. She could not comprehend her colleagues' banter at the operating table, their self-assigned systems of reward and entitlement. The absence of bombardment.

*

Alan was turned away from her; his little torch was on, he was writing in the dark. She touched his shoulder.

'Are you alright?' he whispered.

She had held a gushing aorta in her hands. She had repaired massive damage, one step at a time, concentrating on the tiniest parts of complex systems. In the operating room, she would not let herself think of rescue, only of repair. She had learned that from her mother.

'Do you think my nightmares contaminate our baby?'

He held her with such penetrating gentleness; he should have been the doctor, she thought, not her.

*

A walk on the winter beach, dinner on the sofa – grilled cheddar-and-rocket sandwiches, biscuits from the packet.

'Lukas called,' said Mara.

Time froze.

'He asked Jackie, he managed to get almost the whole team back together – Alice, Amad, Bruno – they all said yes. I told him I had to talk it over with you,' Mara said.

He knew she had already decided.

'One last time,' she said, 'before the baby comes. I'm barely four months – it will be alright.'

Their child, her body.

'I'd stay two weeks, maybe three. Scott will replace me by then. Everything will be alright,' she repeated.

He wanted to smash his head on the floor.

'I'll come home as soon as Scott gets there.'

He went under the blanket so she wouldn't see his face. They'd each spent years calibrating risk in their own way – ever finer, insane distinctions. He lay his head where the dome, slight but firm, was beginning to swell next to her hip bone. Above him, invisible, her face in the dim room.

'Thank you,' she said, his hair a fistful in her hand, 'thank you.' As if she had asked permission, as if she had needed to, as if he had given it.

*

Alan hated airports now. No man's land.

Alan and Peter stood with Mara at the gate.

Peter held his daughter as he always did – as if for the last time. To remember every inch of her, every moment, each goodbye another tree ring of the vascular cambium around his heart.

But Alan held her desperately, which he regretted almost immediately, as soon as she had disappeared through the gate, the howling regret that he had not allowed himself to really feel her, take her in, one last time. They could not see her now, only the surge of people, the entire world, waiting in line behind her.

*

Alan drove Peter home from the airport. They sat in silence in the car in front of the shop. Alan turned off the ignition. The light of the streetlamps ran down the windscreen in the wet snow, falling heavy and huge, dissolving, disappearing.

'Are you sure you won't come in?'

Alan thought of the oblivion of the bottle waiting at home for him in the empty apartment. The familiar metage of misery, stupor, holding on.

'May I come tomorrow instead?'

'Mara was six, the first time Anna went back.'

Driving home, they had both looked straight ahead, past the windscreen wipers and the headlights on the dark highway, and they had been able to imagine, even pretend. But now, they had to look each other in the face, hiding the certainty that they would never see her again.

*

Alan sat at the kitchen table, imagining her in the twilight of the plane, reading her notes, making lists. And floating

in the dark sea of her, their child, who would carry his
father's name or the name of Mara's mother, Anna.

He reached for a glass.

Then the lights went out. Even the little red dot on
the answering machine.

*

Alan stood in the kitchen until his agitation began
to crush him. His panic was a continuous surface, an
endlessly reflecting plane, a Möbius strip or a flexagon,
a Klein bottle, something inescapable, the windows
clattering wildly, he could not tell if it was wind or hail.
Black flak. He took his cap and coat and went into the
street.

The sight of the world stopped him: encased in
ice, nothing forgotten, every detail seized and held
and lit alive. He stood, overwrought with the beauty
and magnitude of it. Glistering power lines weighed
down by the ice, disappearing and reappearing, heavy
silver threads stitching the enamel-hard snow that,
only hours before, had fallen and dissolved with such
poignancy. Within moments, his coat was as stiff as
armour. He would have to take a blow torch to the
zip to get it off, he thought, or melt himself for a long
time in front of the fire.

The phone lines were down. The town was defeated, powerless, electrified by moonlight.

Peter opened the door as if he had known Alan would come after all; Alan stood there as if he had always known they would someday wait for her together.

*

There was a good fire, stoked high – as Mara would have said, 'blaze-worthy'. Alan made his way into the room and saw he was not alone. Two men were sitting in the dark; in their shapeless coats, their hats on their laps, they looked like a symbol of disaster, the bearers of terrible news.

'These are my oldest friends,' said Peter. 'I'm the only one with a fireplace.'

Alan felt his hair dripping onto his shoulders.

'This is Mara's Alan.'

Sandor and Marcus were transformed. They took his hand and beamed at him, Mara's Alan.

*

Peter looked at his friends and at Alan, with his clothes encased in melting ice, hair sopping. They were, he thought, like survivors of a shipwreck: dispossessed, warming themselves by their bonfire on the beach.

*

Alan must have fallen asleep, his face half buried in his collar; when he woke his coat had stopped steaming and was almost dry. He did not want to take it off.

No one noticed he had woken, perhaps Alan himself least of all. He sat watching the fire, shattered, hypnotised, half dozing, bereft. He listened to fragments of their conversation, was lost and listened again, floating in the flow and undertow of their low voices, sometimes unable to distinguish whose words were whose in the dark. What he heard was the luxury of men who had known each other for a lifetime, decades of understanding and misunderstanding, worship and disappointment.

'I understood,' continued Marcus, 'that the woman was to be pitied. But her own colossal conceit made this difficult.'

'All the more reason for pity,' Sandor said.

'Of course,' said Marcus, sadly.

...Each day in that place, Alan thought, you started again, as if you didn't know that luck was a battery being drained, your chances diminishing every minute. As if every day was proof you'd survive the next.

'He had a great sense of irony,' said Peter, 'but no sense of humour.'

'Pure totalitarianist,' Marcus was saying.

… Only a few, Alan thought, had ever been scrupulous in representing both sides.

'Terror can spring from what's most ordinary,' said Marcus.

'Just as love can,' said Sandor.

A log collapsed in the fire.

'Yes,' agreed Peter.

… And the rest believed there was no time left for qualifying right and wrong.

'A young woman came into the shop,' said Peter. 'She told me her name – Helen James – I remember because of course Helena was Anna's mother's name – and she said she was picking up something for her father and handed me a repair slip. I retrieved the parcel from the back – lining repair – and explained I'd used a really good, durable silk blend. I remembered the man who'd brought it in, a few weeks before. In fact, I'd been wondering if he'd forgotten about it. She was taking out her wallet and I showed her that her father had paid for the repair in advance – "I have the receipt here – see – paid in full." She said, "That's his handwriting," and I said, "Yes, your father wrote on the receipt before I had a chance to stamp it; he must be meticulous in his affairs, very commendable." She asked if she could keep the slip of paper and of course I said yes.

'Then she told me her father had died. Only a few days after he'd been here. When she found the ticket in his wallet, she couldn't bear to abandon whatever it was he'd brought in for repair. "In fact," Helen James said, "as soon as I walked into your shop, I knew I'd wear whatever he'd left here." She tried to smile. "Even a top hat." And she took out the cap and put it on – it fitted her perfectly.'

... Where was the place for what he had to say? Alan would spend his whole life telling countless stories with the same ending. An endless story with millions of endings. There was only room, there was no room, for everyone he'd known, for everyone Mara had helped or had been unable to help, the implosive, humiliating intimacy and privilege of knowing someone in the worst moment of their lives.

'What happened then?' asked Marcus.

'She accused me of kindness,' said Peter.

... Few of his closest colleagues, the ones he'd started out with, were still alive – he could not think their lives had been taken for nothing; but he could think it true of his own.

'There's more than one kind of loneliness,' Sandor was saying.

'I don't think so,' said Marcus.

'All the times Anna was away,' Peter said, 'and Mara and I were alone, taught us nothing, prepared us for nothing – it only meant that when Anna died, we never stopped waiting for her to come home.'

Suddenly Alan woke to the fact that Peter's friends had come for Peter's sake and not for their own; that they'd made their way through the storm to be with Peter precisely because it was the ghastly night of Mara's leaving, and they didn't want him to be alone. Now Alan fell into a new kind of listening, the deepest kind – so that 'my father' was his father too, their Mara, his Mara too. Love listened.

*

'Your friend and his father – how did it end?' asked Peter.

'His mother answered the door,' said Marcus. 'Standing there was his father – the father my friend had not seen for half his life and barely remembered. As soon as she opened the door an inch, he pushed past her, never once looking his wife or son in the eye. In that moment, my friend said, his mother had wordlessly agreed to become his father's servant. Within a day, she was kneeling on the floor in front of him, tying or untying his shoes. She was scrubbing the stains from his underclothes, she was cutting his food into small squares and bringing the fork to his lips. He was sick and he had come back to be looked after. For a long time, the son wondered why his mother had let him stay. Then he realised – she let him in the door not because she felt any love or even any pity, but because she wanted to watch him die. And immediately he knew he was wrong – his mother had been a saint. And that terrible thought was his alone, because that was how much he hated him.'

'Does anyone else need a drink?' asked Alan.

The three men, startled from the depths of Marcus' story, stared at Alan as if he'd risen from the dead.

'We didn't know you were awake,' said Peter. 'I'll get us something, or – you know where everything is, I'll help you – I've got a torch, it's really dark in here.'

'Can we help?' asked Sandor.

'I only have one torch,' said Peter.

'We'll stay here and build up the fire then,' said Marcus.

Alan remembered squatting next to a fire built in the scrap of a burned-out car, and the children who would not put down their guns to warm their hands.

*

'How did you all meet?' asked Alan.

Peter explained that Marcus had married a friend of Anna's.

'And Sandor of course,' said Marcus, 'is my little brother.'

'Anna brought us together,' said Sandor.

'Everyone loved Anna,' said Marcus.

'But Anna loved Peter,' laughed Sandor.

They sat in the dark. The fire was low; Alan would force himself up soon to add another log or two. He could barely see the others, heaped in blankets, quiet, whisky-warm. Everyone was thinking, Alan could feel it. Mara would be almost there. Maybe the power would never come back on. Maybe morning would never come.

He wanted to give them all something in exchange for their companionship. Marcus and Sandor had come to save Mara's father and now they were saving him too.

'My father had Alzheimer's,' said Alan. 'I moved into his apartment to take care of him. I did everything for him myself, I wanted to. I was lucky, I could work at home, and there was an older woman who lived across the hall who came when I had to go out to do the shopping.'

'It sounds lonely,' said Sandor.

'He was lonelier than me, he didn't even have himself.'

'And you never thought of giving it up and sending him to an institution?' asked Sandor.

'On the worst days, I thought of it – but only as a fantasy. I would never have done it.'

'But surely you might have?' said Sandor.

'He was my father.'

'My son would lock me up in an instant,' said Marcus, from the darkness on the other end of the sofa.

'I don't have a son,' said Sandor.

'You make it sound like a prison sentence,' said Alan. 'But I loved him, I learned so much from him, all my life, perhaps even the most at the end. He would have done the same for me. It's that simple.'

'It's never that simple,' said Sandor.

'Next you'll be telling us you believe in God,' said Marcus.

'Everyone thinks that memory loss is the end, that it's impenetrable,' Alan said, 'that the whole intricate, intimate world is obliterated – like a painting by a Dutch master, with all its detail, slapped with a fat brush of glossy beige paint, the colour of a hospital wall. For the rest of his life, my father was completely silent. I washed and shaved him, dressed him, fed him. He was almost immobile. Sometimes I took him outside, but he didn't like that. He didn't speak a word. He never showed any sign of recognition or of understanding me, though I continued to talk to him as I always had, talked about what was going on, what I was thinking about. I won't pretend that I wasn't, for a lot of the time, in despair – for his sake. He was empty. And I watched things happening in the world, history happening at a distance, and I couldn't get there. Whatever I was feeling was unimportant compared to what was happening elsewhere, and what was happening to him. I knew very well that my life was not more important than theirs, than his. Had my witnessing saved a single life? Mara at least knows she has saved lives, even if they did not survive the next bombing or the next. When a child survives a long oper-ation, only to die within an hour, when the hospital is blown up...you are surprised to learn that everything matters not less, but more. That, and not the brutality – which never stops being...unspeakable – is the single most important thing I've ever learned.

'One night, I was lying next to my father on the bed, remembering aloud, describing a place he took me to when I was young, a hut by a lake. We arrived late and we swam just before dark. The night was clear and still; the reflection of the stars began to settle into the water; it was as if we were floating in the sky. We couldn't believe the beauty of it. And while I was recounting this to my father, the tears just started falling down his face. After almost three years of what I had thought was vacancy, he reappeared, just like that.

'I thought it was a miracle – but, within moments, he had disappeared again.

'Is hope ever false or futile? His doctor always insisted my father could no longer comprehend. He didn't believe me when I spoke of that incredible moment of lucidity, he shook his head – wishful thinking. But it happened three more times, separated by many months of...nullity, this abrupt appearance and disappearance, this spasm of comprehension and drowning, sometimes in the blink of an eye. And that was the torture of it, that he was still present, still in some way himself. He was his own ghost, aware in a way we can't understand.

'My father had a brother, his only sibling, and when my uncle died, I decided to take my father to the funeral. It was difficult to get there, it was risky, my father did not like to leave the apartment – I wondered if my insistence on going was some kind of self-indulgence. It was a cold day, it took hours to get there; all the while my father stared straight ahead, expressionless, he never looked around, mute and motionless. And that is how he was, throughout the entire service. I sat next to him, knowing I'd made a mistake, put him through an ordeal for nothing. Did I always have to prove a point, to go to the very end, beyond the end? But when the service was over and the attendants were wheeling out the bier, they passed in front of us, and my father suddenly stretched out his arm and laid his hand on the coffin. To say good-bye to his brother.'

There was a long silence. Alan wondered if they wanted to drag him outside and shoot him.

'Do you know about astatine?' asked Marcus, out of the darkness.

'No,' said Alan, 'is it a medicine?'

'An element on the periodic table, number 85. We don't know much about it,' said Marcus, 'because the instant a sample is large enough to see, it vanishes. It appears when uranium decays, its most stable isotopes exist for less than a second – just long enough to detect its existence.'

In the darkness, Sandor remembered watching the shadows made by the swaying trees in his mother's garden on one particular day, not knowing it would be his mother's last; Marcus remembered the silk and scent of a woman's hair, someone he'd known in pharmacy school a lifetime ago; Peter thought of Anna and the gleam of her wedding band, her hand on his thigh; Alan thought of Mara sleeping in the plaster dust in the ruins, and later, looking back, the shadow that remained of them on the floor.

And astatine, the rarest element, reminded Alan of something else: that the mechanism that disproves something is also the very mechanism of proof, and what we do not believe teaches us what we do believe. Faith is a mechanism, just as love is, proving itself, once and for all and again and again, by its disappearance.

'After my father died,' said Alan, 'I went back to the lake where we swam that evening, so many years before. It was an impulse, it was grief, a way to mark the end of all that isolation and intimacy. It was early evening, still light, when I arrived. I walked down to the water. I felt an overwhelming presence, the place itself seemed alive with strangeness. I've been in many situations when my life was immediately endangered. But this was not that feeling, though it was an alertness and a kind of fear. I watched the lake take in the darkness of the sky. No stars. The sense of a presence grew almost overpowering. Then, suddenly, the place was destitute. The presence was gone, though nothing outward had changed.

'I've been in many places where death was present, imminent. But this was immanence. Not mysticism, but mystery. The difference between believing something is true, and knowing it is true, despite oneself. If my father could have chosen any way to convince me of the soul it would have been exactly this way – not by a sensed presence, but by its sudden absence.'

*

They heard the bell on its hinge.

She was soaked, shivering. They sat Mara by the fire. Her father brought blankets, Sandor made strong sugared tea that tasted of woodsmoke.

She was surrounded by Alan and her father and her parents' old friends who had known her all her life, standing over her. She had the sudden image of them leaning over a cradle. Perhaps her own.

'I was waiting for the last connection' – she looked at Alan – 'you know that airport. And then I just – couldn't get on the plane.'

Alan buried his face in her hair. No need for anyone to look away; they were all crying now.

*

They were all asleep by the fire, Sandor and Marcus burrowed under blankets, Mara in Alan's arms. All except Peter, who sat awake at the big table. He couldn't remember the circumference of an infant's head. But he knew he had enough of the weave he wanted, from a place Anna had loved. Pearl-grey stones, the yellow of wild broom.

It had been very hot the weeks before Mara was born; Anna wanted to cool off in the sea. They drove to a village built so close to the beach that the church had been swept away, long ago, in a storm. Anna loved the village and its 'holy water'. She was huge with Mara and lay blissfully in the cold shallows. In the village, there was a little marine museum. Like mysterious figures from a tarot deck come to life, ships' figureheads floated from the walls, their vanished prows cutting through invisible waves, their large unblinking eyes scanning an infinite horizon. The Greeks painted eyes on their boats to see the way forward even in a tempest, and the Phoenicians and the Romans had carved and painted the body entire. Figureheads, the museum placard read, embody the soul of the vessel. 'Everything that floats has a soul,' Anna had said, thinking of Mara inside her. For Anna, the museum was a peaceful place, the figureheads moored in air, bodies and spirits floating free from battle and gale, leaving wreckage and weather behind: a room full of angels, mostly female, midwives ready to deliver a soul safely to shore.

The museum also told the story of a local sailor, who was known to have saved over two hundred men from the sea, before the waves had taken him.

Was rescue always a kind of love? Peter didn't know, and he was tired now; he would leave it to Alan and his philosophers. But he did know, with certainty, that love was always a kind of rescue.

Even when he had no tears left, he would have tears for Anna.

Peter fell asleep at the table, his head in his arms. Sometime in the night, the power was restored. The Anglepoise leaned over him, like a surgeon, like a nurse, like a mother, and held him in a pool of light.

VII

SCEAUX, FRANCE, 1910

The weight of time settled quietly, a slow, massive tilting of trees creaking in the wind, thousands of tonnes swaying gently above their heads. The snow, almost absent-mindedly, drifted down as if it had all the time in the world.

*

Beyond the city, out among the white fields, it could have been any century. It was good to walk at her own pace. The snow fell delicately, just enough to soften Lia's tracks. Her satchel was empty; on the way back it would be filled with kindling and not so easy to carry. Before she was widowed, Lia had been afraid to walk out to the forest alone, but what had once been a kind of destitution had brought its own sore freedom. She was warm in her husband's huge wool overcoat and her own good shawl. She might look eccentric, she thought, but not mad.

At first, in the distance, Lia saw only the camera, like a wooden birdhouse atop its tripod, its bellows and black shroud, and a leather bag open on the ground. Then she saw the photographer disappearing under the black fabric, as if under a woman's skirts.

She stood in the open field at the edge of the forest. They were the only two people for miles. His hair and beard were quartz, grizzled and thick. She thought he might be more than twice her age. It was the camera that interested her. It looked as if it weighed a good twenty kilos at least.

When she was closer, Lia saw that he had domesticated a patch of forest with a thick rough blanket spread out under a tree, a rucksack, a book. He continued working and that was sufficient to make her feel welcome.

Lia looked in the direction the camera was facing and tried to see what he was looking at, why that particular tree, in the whole forest. And then she understood it was the shape of the sky behind the tree that occupied him. And she felt the sudden intimacy of the world, the intimacy between trees and sky, the changing and countless ways they knew each other.

*

'The last time I photographed this place was twenty years ago.'

'Why did you come back?'

'I thought I wanted to see if it had changed.' He smiled. 'But maybe I wanted proof it was the same.'

'I usually photograph the city,' he added.

'Why do you do it?'

He shrugged. 'To keep a record.'

He took another thick blanket from his rucksack and spread it out beside the first, where there was barely any snow. He sat and leaned back against a tree.

After a moment of standing and looking down at him, Lia sat too. It does not take much – a centimetre or two, a word or two – to cross a boundary.

'You don't need a camera to see or to remember,' he said, 'but you need a camera for proof of what is no longer – so that others can remember. I didn't set out to eulogise, but that's what my work has become. Over twenty years, for example, I've captured every detail of the streets of Saint-Séverin, even their demolition, and now all that's been lost survives only on those glass plates.'

Like a lake holding a reflection, Lia thought, even when what it reflects no longer exists.

'I used to come here to rest my eyes,' he said, 'to look at a place I could imagine had been here for millennia and would always be here, though I know this forest will disappear to make way for the city and that the city over there was once forest.'

Lia looked in the direction from where she'd come and imagined the city slowly approaching, like a theatre set on wheels, until it touched the canopy of the trees where they sat.

'I read those books that everyone always talks about,' said Lia, 'by Mr Darwin – well, the first one, and not all of it, I skipped some parts because I was eager to know how it ended.'

He laughed.

'Well, of course I went back afterwards to absorb the science – despite the fact that there's an awful lot about pigeons – and having studied it, I can attest there's nothing in that first book about our coming from monkeys, not in so many words, though the conclusion is undeniable and thrilling – to imagine the light through those prehistoric forests, and the parts of our bodies that were once made powerful by living among those ancient trees – it's something we could even be proud of, as if we had anything to do with it – and Mr Darwin says as much himself, he even uses the word grandeur for that lineage, those progenitors. And the extraordinary expanse of time – it is freedom to think of it.'

He seemed amused. 'Freedom from God?'

'No – well, perhaps. Freedom, at least, from obedience to God. After all, God is not about obedience but about freedom.'

'You've thought a lot about it,' he said.

'My father was a teacher. And I live alone. At night, there's a lot of time to think.'

From the shadows of the trees, they looked out to the fields, a brightness below the solid blue sky.

'I remember when night wasn't a time for thinking,' she said.

'You speak as if that was a time long ago.'

'My husband died.'

She felt a shimmer of wind through the feathered grass above the snow.

'I think we remember someone by living. I think that's the way to remember,' he said.

Lia turned to look at him. He looked younger now somehow. She wondered if she looked younger to him too. The sun felt so warm, where it blazed down between the trees, she almost forgot she was sitting on the cold ground.

'Everyone has ideas,' she said, 'and we have even more ideas when there's someone to listen to us.'

One night, her husband's head still under the covers, he began to talk; he spoke so softly, for such a long time, she could barely hear him, sleep was dragging her away, she was in its warm spell; she sometimes thought her whole life would have been different if she'd heard all he'd said that night.

'I like to take two photographs from the same place in the street,' he said, 'the camera facing one direction, and then the camera facing the opposite direction. Just like when you're in the forest, if you don't turn around and take notice when you're walking, you'll never recognise the landmarks and the turnings on the way back. I was a sailor, and then a soldier, and then I took to the stage – so I've learned a bit about coming and going.'

She had heard that Mr Darwin had taken a thinking walk every day, a long loop around his garden. He liked to keep track of the distance, but did not want to be distracted by having to count the number of circuits he walked. So he kept a pile of stones at the beginning of the path and kicked one aside each time he passed and then simply counted the stones in the new pile at the end. To be lost in thought without losing one's place and without losing one's way.

She imagined the increment of slow change, the patience of a single feature declaring itself over generations, colour seeping into fur, a shape of bone or keratin, carved by time and necessity. The powerful persuasion of use and scale, shade and shape, as if an accumulative wisdom. Everything we see reveals this persistent judiciousness, the winnowing consideration of millennia. The shape of a tooth, a hand; hair, loss of hair; fin, leg, gills, lungs; the slow choice of air or water, light or dimness. Lightning crackling across the infinitely deep canyons of our brains. The formation of our senses embedded in everything we know and feel; the accumulation over millennia of minute perceptions, primordial winters, eclipses, equinoxes, avalanches, harvests, Iron Age rain, the Little Ice Age. And now, animated within her, the splendour of contemplating changes that no one lives to see.

Everything was permanent, nothing was permanent, as if there was only one context where one could use the word indelible – in the span of a single human life.

'Do you have any of your photographs with you that I could see?'

'There may be one or two in my bag.'

She looked at his photographs of streets and shop-fronts, shop windows of mannequins dressed up and waiting for an event that never happens, details of iron-work, staircases, door latches; there were streets she recognised that she knew had disappeared. Every feature of the plangent stillness. She could not tell if the melan-choly was inherent to what had been photographed, or to the photographer, or to the act of photography itself. It was something about possession, she thought, about acknowledging what can never belong to you, how we have no right to that nostalgia, and yet, seeing creates a memory, or confers a memory, or confirms a memory… She would have to think about it later.

'Why are the streets always deserted?' she asked.

'If you hold open the shutter long enough, everything moving disappears.' Or leaves only a trace – a clouding of the air, a thickening of the light, the breath of absence.

She thought several things then. That a photographer's entire life's work would add up to only a few minutes of time. And that one could make a long exposure — say, thirty years of married life, or family life in a kitchen, infants growing to adults — and all that the photographic plate would show was an empty room. But it would not be empty, instead it would be full of life, invisible and real. And then she thought, someday she would look in the mirror and see only the empty room behind her. And then: with a very, very long exposure — say, perhaps, eternity — perhaps we reappear.

*

Where else would the spirit be, but embedded in matter? Why was science so intent on tearing them apart? The spirit evaporates from the body on its own, like water evaporating from seawater, leaving the stain of salt behind. To think of everything as chemical did nothing to dissuade her, it was not a contradiction. Where else would spirit cleave but to matter?

To erase someone from an image does not erase the memory of their having been in that place, does not erase the memory of that person, or that person's memory.

Perhaps memory dies when we do. Perhaps it evaporates, leaving its salt behind.

When someone dies, the very air changes.

She had made her husband a hot bath. She had slipped into the water behind him and held him. He was so thin now. They had sat drowsily together in the steaming water, as they used to, before he was ill. In the span of time it had taken for the water to cool, so silently, so peacefully, leaning against her, he had died. His stillness an inexpressible violation.

*

She knew that she and her husband had had more time at the end than most; she knew it was everything not to die alone, not to be taken brutally, by force. She could never explain, she could never imagine a time when she would be able to explain all he was to her.

Lia had drawn a blanket over him. She had dressed. She had made room for herself and lain down next to him. What could she give him now? She knew what he would want for her: that stillness might grow to peace. Not still: held.

*

The sky was saturating, a deeper blue, darkness rising from within. The snow was beginning to pinken in the fields. She felt the loss – the lifetime of it – of every night without him, of their communication, body to body, even in sleep. Loneliness is not emptiness but negation, with all its agonising precision, its absoluteness; exact, active; in every depth of detail, it is the inverse of love, the dark replica of love.

*

The photographer had two tin lanterns; he lit them and they brought a little heat. Then he took a battered piece of tin from his bag, lined it with branches and, with that small fire, they were warm enough.

He told her about glass plates and shutter speeds, how everyone he cared for had been taken from him when he was still a young man, how he had never made enough money to think of having a family, how he wanted to document everything before it was gone.

Bundled and chaste, she gave herself to the roaming intimacy of their conversation; fears spoken aloud to be discarded; mourning of, gratitude for, all she'd lost. And unsought, unmistakable – inexplicable – she was lit from within by a feeling of bestowal: permission, no, entreaty, to leave her loneliness behind.

*

They spoke their secrets at the edge of the winter forest, in a world of phylum, family, genus, species; in a world where mayflies would appear in the spring – an order 350 million years old, yet with a female lifespan of five minutes and a male, two days. They talked in the long exposure of time – 4.5 billion years of Earth's history – the presence of humans hardly more than a thought. Continental drift, the temperate forests of Antarctica, humid and green; deserts teeming with aquatic life, the arrival of grasslands, of flowering plants, the pillar legs of diplodocus, the emergence of eyes, fins, legs, lungs. Meteor-shocked earth; daybreak to day black, the rain of volcanic glass, forests scorched and flooded; followed by the era of ferns. Alien iridium leaving its trace, the compression of a million years in a centimetre of rock strata. The rime of time crystallising across the ages. The flow of ice growing like stillness. The frozen torrent pushing and pulverising, carrying and crushing, prying and dislodging, picking up and setting down, slow violence and its own slow repair – the wide valleys, the sweet grasses of the upper pastures, rivers settling into their beds. In the expanse of ice, polynya opening like a wound or a well. The weight of the ice shifting like a sea. Glaciers moaning in the darkness.

*

He asked her where she lived and as she spoke they looked across the field to the city, a swamp teeming with life, with its stench and sorrow, its clamour and transcendence. There never was a first man in terms of evolution, but there could, Lia suddenly realised, be a last. And suddenly too, the shocking thought that she herself was not too old to have a child. The possibility rose in her from such a deep place, so long forgotten, as if never known. Perhaps, she thought, a son. Peter, her husband's name, the name his ghost carried. A tenderness took hold of her, a fantasy, a hope. There seemed, in that moment, no difference between tenderness and hope.

*

Lia was suffused with calm when she woke, leaning back against the solid strength of him. The wind had slowed to simple air, and the forest was immense with silence. The distinct winter light, the membrane of blue and blush of late afternoon held the bare branches; the snow, still gentle, floating like stars, added its own silence. But the cold of the ground had seeped into her and the sun was low. There was just enough time to reach home before dark, a beautiful walk in the suspended light of the deepening dusk.

'Will you come home with me? I can make us a good supper.'

Lia thought of him sitting at her little kitchen table. And she thought of the little room beyond, with its narrow bed and lamplight.

The photographer did not reply, perhaps he had fallen asleep too. She turned around to wake him. She was leaning against the tree, only the shape of his weight, the shadow impression of him, like a place a deer has slept, in the snow beside her. Light as a shadow. Then she saw the path he'd taken, his tracks muted then disappearing, as the snow fell in the open field.

*

She imagined him carrying his camera, in its black shroud and almost as tall as himself, over his shoulder, the way one man carries another.

She saw he had filled her satchel with kindling.

*

Slowly, from dusk to dark, the entire landscape changed, as if from within, something like comprehension, like an expression on a face. The sky and the snow began to glow, and the long grasses above the height of the snow, and the trees behind her were monumental as stone. There was no light she loved more than the winter dusk. Behind her, the trees were fretwork, lattice, against the sky, the ancient trees that were also the trees of her childhood.

Longing had never before felt like this, a bright gleam between light and darkness. She had never before understood there could be a purpose to her longing.

The translucent light, almost a kind of knowledge, held her all the way home, darkness falling only as she reached her front door.

Later, unpacking her satchel, she found, like a promise, the photograph he'd left for her. A bridge over a river, lines in the snow: all the paths taken over the course of a day, trails of parting and joining, emerging and merging. And there was something in the photograph that she could not understand or define. Before bed, she held it under the lamp and looked again, still she could not make it out, how the vantage point seemed to be looking back at the bridge from mid-air.

*

Animism tells us that the stone wants to fall, the air wants to move. We are porous, fluid, fleeting, seeking; everything alive responding to the chemistry of light. So many kinds of time.

In the long exposure, the fixed stars leave their trail.

VIII

ESTONIA TO
BREST-LITOVSK, 1980

The first drunkenness of the imagination. The taste of her not yet his. The scent of summer fields through the open window. Nothing visible of her except Sofia's thick gleam of chestnut hair, her brown eyes, her defined jaw, her long fingers and short fingernails; on one finger, a drop of amber set in a band as thin as thread. The stretch of fabric, her coat and his, between them in the swaying train compartment. The press of a strap into the slightest flesh of her shoulder, the resistance of fabric, the hooks, the release of her into Paavo's hands, his mouth. Attunement, boundaries, boundaries crossed. A bare micrometre. The precipice of one word placed next to another, one note next to another. The motion of the train. Light moving through the trees.

*

Sofia was sitting outside the café as if it were not about to rain, slowly sipping her coffee and reading an orchestral score as one would read a book.

She had a face that made Paavo believe in justice, that made him believe she could lead the charge from the ramparts, singing.

*

Paavo wasn't one of them, the painters who came every summer and took over the hotel in the evenings, but he liked their company, their ease with one another. And they, in turn, liked to hear him talk about music, which Paavo defined as pure thought in order to start an argument, and to compare their ideas of the visible and the invisible, and the rules of space and time, so different between painter and composer, yet nonetheless shared. Paavo told them how a score can be like a drawing: Beethoven's multi-dotted semiquavers, each dot adding a fraction of time, his frantic pencil making holes in the paper.

He saw how freely Sofia entered into their conversations, saw her body moving under her clothes. He saw both men and women look at her. Yet, he felt certain they would leave the party together, as if they already belonged to each other. When she went to find her coat and she sought his gaze, he went to find his coat too. As soon as they were outside under the black sky, the trees moving in the wind, his calm vanished; ringing with her nearness, gripping each other like lovers reunited after war, coming together and coming apart at the same time.

*

The party was loud and bright; when Sofia opened the door, the light spilled into the dark garden, and when she closed the door behind her, the darkness rushed in to heal the wound the light had made.

It had been so hot inside. The grass felt cold as snow. In a few moments, the light escaped again across the lawn and Sofia knew he had followed her. The sound of the wind in the trees was the sea.

*

She gripped his hand and he felt the softness at the base of her thumb and, feeling her fingers enmeshed with his, imagined her legs around his waist.

*

They had talked so long, so late, that when they kissed at last, they fell almost immediately to sleep, as if the kiss had knocked them out. A few hours later, light beginning to seep through the curtains, he woke fully dressed, his shirt gathered in her sleeping fist, her bareness abandoned in and out of his clothes – inside his shirt, his sweater, her bare legs burrowed under him, all of her in and out and suddenly awake to his touch.

*

Her evening dress, morpho-blue, small glass buttons glinting, hung from the wrought-iron chandelier, floating in the dimness like a ghost, or a fish in aquarium light. He remembered her inside that glimmering skin of silken light. Then slowly he noticed other things, ordinary details, domestic objects, as if rousing from a dream: the cramped kitchen with its dirty white stove, a plywood table, a faded upholstered chair, a bookcase, a wood and brass metronome.

*

They claimed each other. Knowledge passed between them, simultaneous, aligned, murmuration in an evening sky. As Paavo spoke, he saw the depth of her understanding, his own feelings passing across her face as if in a mirror. They entered a lifetime's conversation, the single conversation with its long silences, repetitions, interruptions; continuous. Everything that was mended and severed by their meeting, everything ignored or given meaning.

They did not notice when the café owner locked the front door and started to sweep the floor around them. Her forgotten tea had steeped to undrinkable blackness. His glass had long condensed, leaving its pale moon on the table.

*

Their flat was always cold. No gas, no hot water; soon there would not even be the memory of these things. Always the same blunt strategy, Paavo thought, to keep us so concerned with staying alive, we forget about living. In the darkness, even with Sofia's mouth to his ear, she sang almost too quietly to be heard. Paavo could put a version of that melodic line in the mouth of a singer in a concert hall – if he erased the poet's words, changed the order of the notes to obliterate the suggestion of a hymn, changed the rhythmic values; that is, if he changed everything. A revision, in every note unrecognisable from the original; satire.

He was learning to alter the ratio of his paranoia; to be less afraid of the committee far away – those who issue the orders – and much more afraid of the enforcers. The more success abroad, the more precarious one's situation; it was a curse to rouse an audience to an ovation. And there was no point in predicting the crime. The usual etcetera dichotomies – drivel, dangerous, sacred, sentimental – were always spiked with something he'd never have thought of, always an element of unpredictability in the offence, the degree of subversion he was charged with; always an uncontrollable element in the vast periodic table of human elements: euphoria, longing, regret, and the worst form of memory, revenge. However, the Composers' Union did allow him to compose soundtracks. This was harmless, they reasoned, no one goes to a film to listen to the music.

They could take away his reputation, his livelihood, they could censor and implicate and banish him. Yet Paavo refused to believe they could stop Sofia singing, naked, entwined, a psalm in his ear.

*

In the concert hall, it surprised even Paavo: the breath-constricting suspense, moving towards the listener and retreating, an excruciating intimacy, the difference between silence that mends and silence that eviscerates, an exactitude evaporating so slowly it was impossible to discern if one was still hearing the notes or listening to empty air. Well, no such thing as empty air. Except perhaps in Antarctica. No, not even there – beyond range of hearing, yet never reaching the zero of complete absence, the eternal trace of a few dozen voices, the sound of a tent breathing in the wind, the wind. Sitting in the last row, his ears broken. No such thing as silence. Silenced; but not silence.

*

Sofia had nightmares: *stranded on an ice floe, lost in a white-out, frozen in the winter sea.*

'You're having these nightmares because the flat is so cold,' Paavo said.

Sometimes, when she woke in the night, the baby, tuned to her maternal wavelength, also woke crying.

'My nightmares never wake the baby,' he said.

But they both knew that was because he hardly slept anymore.

*

Sofia's dreams were full, cinematic, the drama of them plotted to the last detail. She started writing them down, to keep a record.

'Maybe you could sell them as screenplays,' he said.

They always joked in those days, because they were so terrified.

They had become a comedy team, an alloy, stronger that way.

*

The night visitors came at last, in their huge overcoats, and their put-upon attitude that implied that those they had come to accuse, to interrogate, to intimidate, to expel, had a nerve causing them such tedious inconvenience. They took up all the room in the narrow hallway, no room to breathe; they barked or spoke almost inaudibly, with exaggerated solicitude, their great gangster coats seeming to muffle sound, and he realised they were goading him to ask them to repeat themselves, an excuse to say it more than once, muttered like an afterthought. 'Time to leave.'

*

Suddenly, bureaucracy was something that moved at high speed; they were immediately issued the correct documents and ordered to empty the flat. And there were papers and procedures for Paavo's sheet music too, the correct authorisation and stamp, even its own suitcase, for its enforced emigration.

*

Sofia reached for the small notebook and biro beside the bed. *She had chosen that remote place because she had looked at the map and thought no one would find her there. Both the man on the boat and the man in the harbour shop looked her over and saw that her best years were behind her — though, if you looked harder, not unattractive. They'd both thought she'd come to escape some shipwreck or another that her life had become — and both men cast her back, that is, cast their gaze back, to the sea. They weren't right about the wreckage, not exactly. And when she looked at them blankly it was because she did not understand English.*

She now had a new name. She did not know if she was the first, or if she would be the only one, to arrive.

The kitchen in the guest house included a dining area, blue and white tiles on the floor, a long table in the middle of the room, an odd assortment of wooden chairs. Cheerful enough. A menu — a single page, handwritten. Two curtained windows looked out onto the street and the sea beyond. Window boxes with herbs and flowers. She would stay as long as she dared, to see if anyone else came. Each night she left payment in the locked box in the kitchen, for when the proprietress returned. She would always pay in advance, in case she had to leave quickly, no excuse for anyone to care where she went next. The little guest house was hot, silent. From the back door, the sound of insects in the fields. The sea, too far off to be heard.

It would never be possible to know if she was free; she could never live as if she were free. She thought the solitude would be a comfort. But she could barely wait to be hidden in a crowd. She wished she could write a letter so he would know that she had known all along it would come to this, that she had chosen her end; that she would find peace in their revenge.

*

At the border, the train station – sprawling, with turrets and domes like a cathedral – had a hyphenated name, to clarify not that it was both places at once, but neither one place nor the other.

As trains drew out, the ratio of passengers in one place or the other changed incrementally, centimetre by centimetre, until every passenger had crossed the border. And if the train happened to pause halfway, a man without proper documents, sitting in the unlucky seat, could be hacked apart and the fraction of him on the wrong side of the border sent back.

Of course, a man could be severed from himself in other ways.

*

On the stairway of the Composers' Union, the ones who had already begun to teach his classes and take his wages turned away, waiting for Paavo to reach the bottom. But not everyone declined to meet his eye, and what passed between those few, who had long ago become each other's responsibility, was binding; a tableau, fused by a glance. He had only ever known friendship measured in extremity – would he risk his career, his life; would they risk theirs? But now the script had been torn; they each held a piece, they would each play their part. The fated wreck had happened to him, it was his responsibility alone; the wrong text, the wrong language, a scrap of song, a scrap of scripture, praise from the wrong people, other risks he did not know he was taking. But they were still a brotherhood, no need to lift their shirts to compare their scars.

*

Under the immense domed roof of the border station, the ceiling like a glass balloon that could never leave the earth, their suitcases were searched. Books, a baby sweater knitted by Sofia's sister, the sheet music with its exit stamp – the stamp of disapproval – the tape recorder, spools of tape in their flat square boxes.

A border official threaded the tape and they listened. Each note expanded into the vast space above their heads. The crowd seemed to slow to a swell, as if tranquillised. Choral music, his *Magnificat*, his *Dies Irae*, the song he wrote for his sister-in-law, who was not allowed to come with them. The music made a mystery of that filthy place, note by note the echo of something unspoken, the truth we are sometimes able to perceive only as a mirage or, further still, something beyond the spectrum of human sight. *There is only one language for each pair of souls. Others eavesdrop but do not understand.*

The border police tossed the tapes back into the suitcase; they confiscated the baby sweater. How canny of them, a flash of perception, to seize what was irreplaceable.

*

When we are moved, Paavo thought, when we feel something beyond us, it is the boundary, the limit of the body that allows us to recognise it. Limit is proof of the beyond. Not the self, but what lies beyond the self. He would not be surprised if physics made sense of it someday; but only because science is bent on proving it doesn't exist. Scientists will rip us to shreds looking for it, but it will not be found where they are looking. He remembered a joke, about someone who'd lost something and was searching across the street, under a streetlamp. Why are you looking for it there? Because the light is better.

Now he thought perhaps it was not a joke after all. Don't look for something where you've lost it, you'll never find it there. Look where the light is.

We need to perceive, he thought, according to the scale that matter insists upon. There is the body and everything that is not the body, but at the highest magnification we are one system; how else could sound waves dismantle us, free us, bind us? Here, inside the cavernous hall of the Brest-Litovsk station; while someone could be standing outside the immense stone building and not hear a thing.

Paavo looked at the border patrol guard and thought about all that was sealed behind her scowl, all the mothering and daughtering she had done, the lovemaking; he saw her eyeing the baby's sweater, admiring the complex pattern, made with the thinnest gauge needles and wool, which had been knitted with such care and love, as if its innocence could survive in the world. He saw her thinking that she might take the sweater and give it to her grandchild, thus proving what she was paid to deny every working day – the value of such a bond. Innocence and trespass. With every tightening of the screw, the tyrant makes our hope more precise. And nothing enrages a tyrant more than hope.

*

It was the same nightmare, always. Sofia could not purge it from her sleep. Eventually she recounted it to Paavo;

there was no need to whisper now, but it was a hard habit to break.

*

She was walking behind them, they were not far ahead, perhaps ten metres, when they disappeared. She turned her head to look up and down the beach, which made up the entire world in this place, fifty kilometres in either direction. They had disappeared but she could still hear their voices amid the immense crash and draw of the sea. Well, it wasn't their voices, only Paavo's, patiently explaining something their son, Aimo, six years old, couldn't follow. Inexplicably, she could hear him clearly above the roar of the waves. She caught up and saw where they had dropped to. The coast had been eaten away from underneath, a lip of rock that had been scooped out by the sea, a gradual edge, and then a more rapid drop until the beach hung a good seven or eight metres above the waves, disappearing them from view like a ha-ha. She followed, sliding down beside them, and turned to see the beach was gone, the view blocked in reverse, with nothing but the wall of rock at their backs.

The sea, wide and slow from the beach above, was terrifying from the strand below, thousands of miles of unpredictable force, moving in and out, a consuming restlessness. Already the sand behind them was no longer a few steps up, but a cliff, and they would have to retrace their steps a long way to be able to scramble back up; the remaining rim of beach seemed shorter now, melting as she watched. She caught up with them and grabbed their son's hand. She yelled against the wind that they had to go back. 'The tide, now.' And then she ran, with Aimo's small hand in hers, hard going in the soft sand and the rising water. Paavo looked about, unconcerned, and turned back to her, smiling.

She had a memory of someone holding their son, Aimo, when he was two weeks old, how that man had walked out to the balcony and leaned over, absently holding their precious son over the edge. And how someone had once slammed a car door barely a centimetre from Aimo's two-year-old head.

Her breath burned through her. She looked behind to where Paavo was gazing with indifferent astonishment at the immensity of the sea. She shouted, begged him, but even she couldn't hear her own voice now. Finally, she reached a place where the edge of the beach was still climbable and she lifted Aimo and climbed up after him, no strength to spare. Now she saw how much of the beach had been swallowed, and saw too that they were still not out of danger, and she urged Aimo to run with her, inland, towards the blurred line of trees in the wind. Already they were losing their advantage and they did not stop running until they reached the sea wall and climbed the steps. She realised now she had not stopped screaming for Paavo all the way.

She found her binoculars in her bag and saw he was laughing — at her. Defiant and amused at what he considered her maternal perception of danger. Then he waved her off, dismissed her, a gesture she hated. She scanned the beach to see if there was anyone who might help her, to convince him to get moving, but the beach was empty. She continued to watch through the binoculars, waving and shouting at him, despite his disregard. And then, she saw his head turn sharply and when he turned towards her again, she saw, in the small glass of the binoculars, how his face had changed. The alarm in the shape of his mouth. At last he began to run. But the place where the edge of the beach was still low enough to be climbed had been swallowed by the sea, the beach up to the sea wall completely overtaken by the tide, and the harder he swam towards the wall, now barely visible, a darker line like a vanishing pencil mark on the deepening sky, the farther away he found himself. Now the light was also going fast, grainy with darkness as if the sky too was losing to the sea, a faint pink filling the spaces in the dark, then quickly being soaked up like blotting paper. Above, the first star hardened against the deepening night and the sea slammed and suddenly thrust him away. In an instant, he seemed miles from shore. She continued to look, the binoculars pressing against her cheek, though she could no longer see him. At that moment, Paavo saw the entire coast disappear; as if he did not know the moon took hold of the sea every day, as if she had not thrust the tide chart into his hand every day since they'd arrived, as if he did not know how quickly darkness descends, as if he did not know perfectly well one can drown simply by standing still. She looked out at the dark sea as it surrendered to the turning world. Far off, white crests flickered and vanished in the almost-blackness. She was sobbing now, out of fury, she had been

*warning him about the tide forever. At that moment, it was
fury, fury, fury that possessed her, as mother and son held each
other and looked out. Looked and looked for any sight of him.
Countless times they thought they saw Paavo climbing the sea
wall, but it was not him, not anyone. Later, she thought maybe
it had been a trick of the distance, the growing darkness, that
made it seem she could see him, kilometres away in the waves,
or climbing over the sea wall. Even as she watched, she knew
it could not be; it could not be, as she waited, looking ahead
enraged, looking behind in hope. They stood there looking out,
little Aimo cold and crying, as the stars bloomed into sight,
countless, flung like salt, above the consuming indifference of
the sea.*

*

After Sofia recounted the dream to Paavo, she never had
to dream it again. But still, it did not quite leave her, she
was afraid of it, hovering within range; like a nightmare
of looking out a plane window at 30,000 feet and seeing
a face.

Paavo's explanation seemed true to her – that she had
kept dreaming it not because of the terror, but so she
could wake each time and find him next to her, after all.

IX

RUE GAZAN, PARIS, 1908

Our beautiful spring day. The glorious flower meadow, the armful you carried home for us, Eugène, filling the huge heavy glass vase so that the thirsty marsh marigold, mahonia and broom in all their shining yellows could drink and drink the singingly clear cold water.

That evening, I could not comprehend that the wildflowers you'd picked for us had outlived you.

On your wrist, the second hand of your new watch was lurching forwards, though your pulse had stopped.

*

I had never arranged a funeral before, I only knew I could not bear to have any flowers on your grave.

*

It must have been unbearable to be pressed against the air, hearing me shouting for you, not being able to answer. Neither of us

189

fluent then in the language of the dead. But now, my ears and eyes never miss a sign you send me: a flicker of light between the trees, a twitch of wind across my face, a bird sitting for long minutes on a branch beside me, unafraid. I hadn't understood before, how being unafraid makes room for love.

*

Ernest Rutherford and his young wife were in Paris and we were all invited for dinner at Paul Langevin's that beautiful June night in 1903 to celebrate Marie Curie's doctorate. We had moved outside for coffee in their peaceful garden overlooking Parc Montsouris, and it had grown dark and Pierre Curie brought out his lantern — a copper tube bathed in a solution of radium and zinc sulphide — faintly glowing among the leaves like the perfect flesh of a lover one only imagines. Perhaps it was that earthly light or all the talk of Madame Palladino and the levitating table, but I have always remembered the feeling I had, listening to the Curies that night — the shiver, my first realisation that nature, in that new lantern light, could contain something that seemed so alien, something that was impossible to say whether presage or promise. And it was one thing to think about the elements in stone or pitchblende, the radiant heart of inanimate matter, and even a spiritual radiance inside the material human body, but quite another to think of the concomitant: that there might be, in the abstract world, in the domain of the dead, the remnant of desire — the persistence of longing in a phantom body — to feel an apple in the hand, to feel the heat of the sun and the cold of the sea, to taste the salt of the sea on the lips of another, to be opened and held. Alas, that the dead might remember. I had never considered this possibility before. At the séances of Madame Palladino, the investigating scientists had bound the medium's arms and held her hands, they pressed down on her feet with their own, they insisted the room remain light enough to scrutinise her every movement. Pierre Curie described how they had measured the muscle contractions of her limbs with sensitive instruments while objects flew about the room; they monitored acoustical vibrations, electrical and magnetic fields; they used electroscopes and compasses and galvanometers to analyse objects moving at a distance — yet still Madame Palladino held the very air with her powers, and the table rose, and an invisible force parted the curtains, and no one, not all the intelligence of l'Académie, could detect deception. In the darkened room of the séance, there had been both the scent of the hunt — the avarice of science, its conflation of knowledge and control — and the satiety of inexhaustible mystery. I listened to them all and could not make up my mind — Pierre Curie was particularly persuasive, pleading that science must never foreclose what it does not understand. And who could speak for the dead, who could prove if they knew or felt, or what they knew or felt? Whether one believed or not in such manifestations — self-motivated objects, telepathic messages, hauntings — the truth was untouchable. The laws of nature *would exert their will, regardless. And, I thought, if observation changes the phenomenon, how can we know anything?*

In that hot summer garden, among the branches of the trees, the radioluminescent tube continued to glow with its cold fire. I found myself standing next to Marie Curie. Perhaps it was because I told her that the glow of her radium — not in its colour but in its magic — reminded me of how breath becomes visible, turning white in the cold air, as if we could see what's unspoken, see even silence; perhaps because I was a woman mathematician and I reminded her of her dear British friend Hertha Ayrton, or simply because it was such a welcome novelty to speak woman to woman, she confessed to me, in a whisper, that she was pregnant. As we stood there, smiling at each other, the lit moon came out from behind a cloud, moving slowly across the sky like a planchette.

*

All the time, Eugène, I stood in the Langevins' garden, listening to the others talking, all the time that I was imagining the distant glow of radium in the depthless black cauldron of pitchblende like small voices of phosphorescence calling weakly from the bottom of the sea, and imagining the luminosity of souls floating above a séance table; even as I was thinking about the fact that the very act of perceiving alters what we see, you were watching me; until the world changed from a place where I hadn't known you existed to a place where you would always be alive. After the party, we crossed the street together and peered down into the rustling world of Parc Montsouris. I'm used to negotiating the practical and the abstract, but at that moment, in that quiet street with you, I could not determine why I should say goodnight or ever again make my way home alone.

Already I longed to be consumed with fascination by the ordinary life of your body, to drown in every thoughtless detail and gesture, how you held a glass, or a pen or a fork and knife, whether you opened and read a magazine from the front cover or the back. It was the vertigo I had longed for always, that there be no end to my falling, no boundary to knowing and loving another. No brick wall of time, no dead end of betrayal, boredom, selfishness. How is it possible to perceive this potential, the beautiful irrealis mood, in the endless space of a few moments? And yet, I did know it: the wild certainty that you held the secret of my future.

And then we began to walk, rue Gazan, avenue Reille, as if inhabiting the same dream, and began a conversation the way we would later share the same calendar pages, flowing between your handwriting and mine, together recording our days; and the invisible ink of our nights. You told me, in your gentle, wondering way, about the moment you realised you wanted to spend your life studying the world, when you were fourteen, staying with your uncle and cousins in the foothills of the Carpathians; you told me of places I knew nothing of, about the birch groves, the poplars, the willows, the cornfields and windmills of Mazovia; the smell of the resin in the forest near

Gdańsk; watching the cows swaying through the mist to drink at the River Brok; the picnics at Marki, Sklody, Salzbrunn, Silesia, dressing up and dancing, laughing and talking in your mother tongue, and your astonishment at the vast libraries in those country houses without a single book in the language of the oppressor.

You took Sandor and Marcus and me to see some of those places — the world of your childhood; later, you said you never wanted to return again, as if everything you had known had become a lie — because history, you said, changes the past, not only the future.

Marcus begins to bury his feelings in loneliness, but little Sandor is still sweet and open as always, still cries when something is wrong, still reaches for his older brother's hand. You were right, my wise love, to believe they would look after each other — not half-brothers, but brothers.

When we were first married, you worried I'd feel abandoned if you turned away from me in your sleep. You placed your hand on my heart and said: no matter what direction we face, you are on my left side and I am on yours.

Until the night we met, I had never imagined that — on either side of the boundary between breath and death — our longing, alas, alas, might be the same.

X

HIGHCLIFFE, DORSET, 1912

Hertha sat on the beach at Highcliffe like a stone god, beautiful, substantial, knowing; while Marie lay at her side, a heap of rags, a wraith, an offering. Marie had been sacrificed to the mob, and Hertha knew what it meant to be given shelter. They had ravaged her, Hertha thought, stripped her friend clean, left only this skeleton behind, asleep at last on a blanket beside her while the non-repeating, non-terminating sea came in and in. Loyal Miss Manley watched over the children, happy to think of the battle-worn Madame Marie Curie at rest. You could see the women Marie's daughters would become, Hertha thought, each reflecting a side of her friend, the intransigent and the playful, like two elements, separated and distilled. Marie's daughters would live beyond them, they would change the world, they would avenge their mother and all women who were perceived as a body or brain but never a soul. They would avenge Hertha's own suffragist daughter, at that very moment locked up in Holloway prison for protesting. They would never stop saying what was right. Marie's dress and shawl rustled in the breeze, but Marie slept on, minimal, lifeless, like something cast aside, left behind. My God, thought Hertha, looking down at her friend, what they have done to you, simply for being in love. Marie was a little warrior in a military camp run by men, she would always have to prove herself. How tired we all are, Hertha thought, of persistently needing to say what is right.

Miss Manley came to tell them it was time for supper. Shall we wake Madame? No, said Hertha, let her sleep, let her sleep, I'll stay here with her until she wakes. Leave something warm for us. And Miss Manley, smiling in perfect agreement, nodded.

Marie had once told Hertha that she kept a tiny amount of radium in a jar next to her pillow. Awake in the night, she could lie in bed, bathed in the moon-light she had discovered in the pitch. No one had really believed it was there. Except Pierre, of course. But it had been she, with her Bohemian pines, who had stood stirring her cauldron all those weeks in the snow.

Now, Marie had crossed the Channel at Calais unseen, veiled and travelling under her own maiden name, Maria Skłodowska – proof, if any were needed, that truth is the only disguise needed in a corrupt world. The Paris newspapers were already measuring the size of her head and features in an attempt to expose racial malignancy, she was now the foreigner, the degenerate infiltrator who, they said – it could now be nothing but abundantly clear – had also robbed her dead French husband of his rightful title as the sole discoverer of a new element; and whose single-minded ambition in coming to France had been to become a manipulative widow bent on luring a once-saintly husband from his saintly wife. And finally, about your second Nobel Prize that you have won, Mrs Curie – we ask that you, in your state of shame, do not accept or attend the reception. Langevin had written to the papers in her defence, fought duels to restore both their honour, but it was too late, always too late, the moment wolves taste blood.

But now – Hertha had arranged everything – they were all to spend August together, secreted and safe at Highcliffe; at last, Marie's daughters could be with their mother, without harassment, in a disused mill house in the forest of Chewton Glen. They had all done well, no one knew where they were, Hertha was sure of it, and her friend could regain her health in both the quiet of the forest and the sea air. Their very being there, undiscovered, was spit in the eye of the oppressor. And Hertha knew there was no medicine more important than knowing there was someone in the world who knew the very heart of you and would protect you. Without irony, Hertha thought, mothers of all lands, unite.

There had been only one moment of disquiet.

They had stopped at the pharmacy one evening, on the way home from the beach, to see if they could find something to help Marie sleep.

The shop was empty of customers. The pharmacist was reading a newspaper. He looked up and Hertha explained what they needed.

'Is this for yourself?' the pharmacist asked.

Hertha detected an accent.

'No,' said Hertha, 'for my friend.'

He looked at Marie then, and Hertha suddenly knew they had encountered the only French pharmacist in all of Dorset.

'There are tisanes that can work well for your friend,' the pharmacist said quickly.

He steered them to a shelf and selected a tin. 'It's perfectly safe,' he said, looking at Hertha and not at Marie. 'I would suggest this remedy to my own mother. I take it myself. And the simplest remedy is often the best.'

Hertha nodded.

'I'll give you a sample to try. If it works for your friend, you can come back for more.' He wrapped the tin in paper and handed it to Hertha.

'No charge,' he said.

'To whom do we owe this kindness?' asked Hertha.

'My name's Marcus – but I'm just the locum, I usually work in a shop up north.'

He wished them goodnight and they stepped back out into the street. It was late now and the wind from the sea was cold. While they were inside the shop, Marie's hand, clutching, had never left the crook of Hertha's arm. Now Hertha felt her friend's grip relax. Marie looked at Hertha with a tentative smile.

'Perhaps he didn't recognise you at all, perhaps he was simply being kind,' said Hertha.

But they both knew they had been discovered.

'One could make up a thousand stories to explain this kind chemist,' said Marie.

'As one could,' agreed Hertha, 'for the kindness of any stranger.'

'Perhaps he knows what it is to flee scandal, perhaps he came here because he fell in love with an Englishwoman, perhaps she – or he – was already married when they met…' said Marie.

'Perhaps he's a widower,' said Hertha, 'though he looked quite too young.'

They walked on, Marie still holding Hertha's arm.

'Do we really need our own misery to teach us to be kind?' asked Marie.

'I think perhaps we might,' said Hertha.

'That's a dark thought,' said Marie. She hesitated. 'I won't believe it.'

The sea air was doing its work, Hertha thought. Marie was never going to give them the victory of her bitterness. She had already stepped halfway out of their mirror.

It took them only a few minutes to walk to the end of the village and it would be only a short walk back to the mill house through the trees.

Just before they entered the path into the woods, they stopped and turned for a last look at the sea. One could never separate moonlight and sea – light from its reflected surface – or even, of course, moonlight and the moon. Just as one could never separate the moon from the tides or from the force that acts on them both. Force always exists, whether two animate or inanimate things hold each other, or something animate holds something without will or desire – an apple in the hand. The sea is so old, almost as old as the earth, Hertha thought, and the moon, how old was the moon? They would know the answer someday; and there were so many other things she wished she could calculate herself, like the probabilities in seemingly random patterns in nature, like patterns made by the sea on the sand… But, for now, there were other, more urgent jobs to be done.

'What are you thinking about?' Marie asked.

'Force,' said Hertha.

'Someone will get to the bottom of it someday.'

'Or get to the top of it,' said Hertha.

It felt good to laugh. They were still young enough – yet, such old friends.

They would read to the girls before bed, and then read to each other, until Marie closed her eyes.

'Thank you,' Marie said, 'for suggesting that I come.'

'You were right to come,' said Hertha.

'*You* were right.'

They laughed again.

'Only a woman scientist would think of stirring a pot for months,' said Hertha.

'Stirring it up,' said Marie.

They took one last look at the sea. One could almost believe Paris did not exist.

'You'll see,' said Hertha, 'young women will know you're wonderful, they'll understand – precisely – why we must insist on love.'

Marie shook her head.

'Even your daughters,' said Hertha. 'Even Pierre.'

And that's when Marie began to cry.

Hertha held her friend, and the salt wind and the green of the forest held them both.

'I was a fool,' said Marie, 'to think I'd find that kind of happiness twice.'

Hertha had consoled women all her life; she had given shelter, she had been given shelter. She was seven when her Polish father died. She had helped her mother raise her seven siblings. Hertha had a daughter and an adopted daughter. She was a fighter for the rights of women and had nursed hunger strikers back to life. She knew the different kinds of tears women cried, and understood the specific tears Marie cried now, which were not about finding happiness twice, or even about humiliation, or rage at injustice; but because there is a moment when a woman believes she has lost her last chance. The great mourning in a life.

'It was because you'd known happiness that you could believe in it,' said Hertha. 'When have you ever given up when you believed in something? They want us to make that bargain, always that same bargain, against ourselves – one part of us at the expense of another. Of course we must prove them wrong. And if we fail, it is still the right thing to do. And besides,' she added shrewdly, 'you went to Sweden and sat across from the king and no one could stop you.'

They were almost back. They saw the light in the windows. The sky above the trees was saturated with stars. Maximum solute. A map of time.

They stood for a moment before going inside.

Hertha thought of the fall of Babylon, how the priests remained alone in the empty city to continue their work, faithfully recording the changes they observed in the heavens. They had kept watch for years, until, eventually, the stars and planets revealed a mathematical order. Is it belief that leads us to perceive an order, or order that persuades us?

She thought about the famous astronomical clock in Prague, 500 years old, with its skeleton brandishing an hourglass — dust to dust, the sands of time — and how those early clocks, like the church bells that rang their dedication to eternity, marked cosmic time, the largest order of the turning world and its seasons; not the limited commodity that time had become, the minute calibrations of the factory and workhouse. She thought of the imprisoned suffragist hunger strikers and the government's ruthless calculation, counting the days before releasing their prisoners at precisely the last moment, so the women wouldn't become martyrs to the cause.

'I don't want to think about clocks when I look at the sea and the stars,' said Hertha. 'I want to think about the unceasing and the infinite, an endless line flowing into the future, or at least cycles that are so large we will never grasp them. But…here I am, thinking about clocks and time running out.'

Our machines govern our behaviour, thought Hertha, but they will never teach us meaning.

Is meaning at the heart of behaviour, or is behaviour at the heart of meaning? Science must never confuse the two, or the behaviour of matter with motive; meaning lies beyond the reach and intent of science. Science can never determine if there is something beyond flesh and bone because that inquiry is inadmissible.

'What are you thinking about?' asked Marie.

'Flesh and bone,' said Hertha.

'I didn't think of the dead when I saw Becquerel's X-ray,' said Marie. 'I didn't think of skeletons in the ground. I thought: these living bones are the beloved hand of his wife.'

They had always talked this way, a drifting conversation, like two sisters lying in bed at night, whispering in the dark.

Steam rises from the stirred pot. The microbial world receives our bones. Perhaps meaning lies in the change of state, thought Hertha. The purpose of synapses is the space between them; meaning is in that gap. How old is starlight? There is always a gap of time between an object and our seeing it – just as we cannot see the stars and just as we do not exist, Hertha thought sadly, to those who might see our starlight.

Women never sleep, thought Hertha.

'No time to sleep,' said Marie.

*

In the Highcliffe pharmacy, Marcus went back to his newspaper and looked at Marie's face. He wanted to take her hand and tell her he had visited Poland when he was a child; that he had a Polish father and a French mother; he wished he had spoken his dead father's name aloud and had told her that Eugène had been born in the Tatras. He longed to tell her that he wished her well.

*

Later, Marie would bring out her diary and write to Pierre, and Hertha would write to William. They were the Polish pair, Hertha thought, writing to their dead; women of science, physicists' widows, whose adored husbands had always been alert to new ideas, and never pretended to drift off when something important had to be said, and who had even shared an appetite for listening. Such love was triumph. They would write as women have always written: late, by lamplight, the children asleep.

XI

CAPTAIN'S WOOD, SUFFOLK, 2010

Whenever Helen James walked in the woods she wore her father's cap, its soft lining repaired as good as new, the impeccable repair her father had never had the chance to enjoy. The lining was still perfect, a silk blend, she recalled, amply durable, lasting all this time.

Sometimes Helen sang when she walked. Everything listens when you sing, she thought, everything sings when you listen.

Sometimes she turned and her father was next to her, so close that if he were alive she would feel his breath in her hair. She still longed for him; but his quiet presence, when it came, did not feel conjured by her longing. She did not need to name it or explain it. She knew that humans have felt this always; as simple as seeing deer at the edge of the forest, or knowing it has snowed overnight by the change of light in the bedroom when you wake, something ordinarily perceivable. No need to explain it any more than one needed to explain any of our senses — hearing, or tasting, or feeling the wind. The slow evolution of perception: the first vertebrates to move from water to land, beginning to grow what would become eardrums, detecting low frequencies as vibrations in their heads; the photosensitive patch evolving into the pinhole eye and socket, from light-sensitive sponges to the eye cup of the *Tripedalia cystophora*, the diversity of mollusc eyes, birds with their four visual pigments, their astonishing distance acuity, a flicker fusion ratio to detect the motion of the sun and moon crossing the horizon. When we grew eyes did others of our kind believe us mad for what we saw? Perhaps it simply begins like this: always, just as she reaches the same turn of the path where it bends into the trees, his hand finds hers.

XII

THE GULF OF FINLAND,
2025

A field becomes a battlefield; becomes a field again. Words rise on thermal fax paper, a thousand kilometres from where they were written. A man manufactures bone music of the banned. Truth, where regret begins, is a slightly paler shade of dark than defeat. The Baltic Way, a human chain of 2 million people, over 675 kilometres long, spanning three countries, stands in solidarity for fifteen minutes. The snow is slightly darker than the sky. The bombs fall. A man who survived one war dies in another. Quietly, a pool begins to form where no water has been for 34 million years. Bacterial flagella go about their microscopic business. Nightfall. Murmuration, like smoke, twists in the sky as light surrenders to the turning world. The sea bulges under the moon. Someone moves in their sleep, making room for another. Someone reads, someone stirs a pot, somewhere rain hammers tin gutters, reminding a man of childhood storms and monsoons he'd read about in books. The thief, moonlight, picks up every object on a bedside table, fingers it and pockets it; the room goes dark. At a small desk next to a bed, a woman contemplates causal sets, spacetime, scale-free correlations, while a child grows inside her. All the ways we lie down in a field.

*

We think of history as moments of upheaval when forces converge, the sudden upthrust of the ground we're standing on, catastrophe. But sometimes history is simply detritus: midden mounds, ghost nets, panoramic beaches of plastic sand. Sometimes both: a continual convergence of stories unfolding too quickly or too gradually to follow; sometimes, too intimate to know. Someday, a geologist will identify the centimetre of rock strata that will prove Antarctica was once covered in ice. Someone will find the flag that once flew at the South Pole, washed up on an equatorial beach. History is liminal, the threshold between what we know and can't know; land and sky a single coordinate plane in the mist. The one who rescues the rescuer. Terminal lucidity. The few kilometres, a turn of the head, between surplus and famine. Surgery by the light of a car battery. Stars invisible in daylight.

*

Aimo saw her enter the café with the pyramid-shaped cakes in the window and mismatched tables, chairs, cutlery and crockery; the entire café like a mnemonic of every meal they'd shared.

Perhaps Anna was meeting someone, or had just stepped inside to order one of their famous cakes. He waited across the street but she didn't reappear. Perhaps she was sitting at a table by herself, with a latte and a book, waiting for someone — here, in their café, where he'd fastened the necklace with the chain that happened to bring the pearl to rest perfectly between her breasts as if he'd measured the chain with his desire. He waited, but still she didn't emerge. Soon he risked going to the door and looking in. She was at the bar, reading, the steaming cup, her scarf and handbag beside her, the handbag he'd bought for her in Amsterdam on the Queen's birthday, the entire city laying out its wares, an epic jumble sale, it cost almost nothing but it was meant for her, the brown leather so soft, folded like an envelope, the faded silk lining the colours of an autumn forest; it fit her hand as if made for her, like everything she wore, a collection of beloved items found in markets and second-hand clothing shops, the silk shirt, the tweed jacket, half a suit, everything from the last mid-century, the faint scent of perfume at the collar that made it hers, everything ready to slip off, to be stepped out of, to be pulled up, pulled open, unfastened, slipped through, unbuttoned, unclasped, left clasped, unclasped again.

*

When Anna came out at last he did not intend to follow her; he knew the swing of her arms, the length of her stride, the slight brushing of her thighs in her dark tights; he fell in readily and familiarly with the speed of her body, and that is why he did not catch up with her.

She entered a shop – to buy a certain kind of drawing paper – he remembered this – and when she left the shop, again he was unable to close the distance between them.

*

The long fuse of memory, always alight.

*

Aimo followed her through the streets of the old city, across the square with its domed church, into the park. A cold spring evening. Rain-black trees.

Dusk, the last light; no, not the last.

He was afraid he would remember only enough to wish for her and not enough to find her again.

Someday Anna would come to understand that everything she had thought of as loss was something found.

The city streets grew indistinct then brightened again with artificial light.

She turned to see if he was following; like something moving at the edge of a forest, not quite seen.

*

His hair was thick, spiky, a handful, a place to hold on; his face lined, strong-boned. He had the look of one who had been loved, but not in a long time.

She knew a woman who fell in love with a face in an advertisement when she was fifteen. He did not look at all like him, but there was something about him that reminded her of that story and how one could fall in love with a photograph as if it were the memory of someone.

The door opens; in the hillside, at the sea's edge, in a small city garden, in a café where she sits reading while the snow falls. Frost like tulle across the fields, the smell of tobacco on an empty beach.

He pulled on his bulky sweater and his open satchel across his shoulder. Aimo forgot his book on the café table, Anna saw and ran after him. He thanked her, they parted and walked away. Then, pierced with that long-ing, the belonging that no one can ever explain, they both turned, and looked back.

*

The snow falls, inventing its own silence.

*

Who can say what happens when we are remembered?

ACKNOWLEDGEMENTS

Mid-sea, I heard the mountain birches;
in the salt-wind, your voice in the trees.

My very special thanks, longstanding over the decades, to Alexandra Pringle. Thanks to Jared Bland, Diana Miller, Roberta Mazzanti, Stephanie Sinclair, Ruta Liormonas, Heather Sangster, Jennifer Griffiths, Kimberlee Kemp, Allegra Le Fanu, Elisabeth Denison, Janis Freedman Bellow, Eve Egoyan, david sereda, Seán Virgo, Gareth Evans, Simon McBurney, Andrew Wylie, Tracy Bohan, Nigel Newton, Kristin Cochrane. And, always and ever, to Rebecca and Evan.

The quote on page 113, 'Every angel is terrifying', is from the first elegy of Rainer Maria Rilke's *Duino Elegies*, translated by Stephen Mitchell.

A NOTE ON THE TYPE

The text of this book is set in Perpetua. This typeface is an adaptation of a style of letter that had been popularised for monumental work in stone by Eric Gill. Large-scale drawings by Gill were given to Charles Malin, a Parisian punch-cutter, and his hand-cut punches were the basis for the font issued by Monotype. First used in a private translation called 'The Passion of Perpetua and Felicity', the italic was originally called Felicity.